ORDER AND CHAOS

A SHORT STORY ANTHOLOGY

BREAKTHROUGH BOOK COLLECTIVE

First published in Great Britain in 2023 by Breakthrough Books.

Ebook ISBN: 9781739379360

Print ISBN: 9781739379353

The rights of Eli Allison, Mark Bowsher, Stephanie Bretherton, Jamie Chipperfield, Sue Clark, Jason Cobley, Stevyn Colgan, Samuel Dodson, Miles Hudson, A.B. Kyazze, Pete Langman, Virginia Moffatt, Eamon Somers, Nicole Swengley, Damon L. Wakes, PJ Whiteley, to be identified as the authors of this Work have been asserted by them in accordance with the Copyright, Designs and Patents Act 1988.

Cover design by Eli Allison.

No part of this book was produced using generative AI.

CONTENTS

'To doubt everything, or, to believe everything, are two equally convenient solutions; both dispense with the necessity of reflection.'

— HENRI POINCARÉ

SONGBIRD AND STATUE

DAMON L. WAKES

I n days before the dawn of time, two gods struggled for control over all that was. One was named Order, who strove above all for stillness and perfection. The other was named Chaos, who strove above all for motion and change. When Order set the spheres upon their paths, Chaos sent out comets to knock them astray. When Order called land out from the water, Chaos tore it asunder. These gods fought ceaselessly, yet they had formed from the void as twins and each was as strong as the other.

'This battle is futile,' said Order one day, after countless aeons of struggle. 'We must settle our differences by some other means.'

'For once we are in agreement,' Chaos conceded. 'But what do you propose?'

Ten millennia passed while Order considered its challenge.

'We should each of us set a great work upon the mortal plane. To these works shall our fates be bound. Whichever lasts the longest, its maker—victor, sole survivor—will have won dominion over all the world.'

Ten millennia more passed while Chaos deliberated.

'I accept,' it said at last, 'but as you were the one to set the challenge, you must be the first to act.'

This time, Order did not hesitate, for it had long considered what its work would be.

From the depths of the earth, Order called up a pillar of flame. The skies grew black with smoke, and the cunning of the craft was revealed only by the sparks that smote the trees. The people of the earth dropped their spears and threw themselves down before the spectacle, and in that moment they swore to serve their first and only god: for Order's likeness had been left upon the land in stone one hundred cubits high.

Order smiled from within the statue. To act first should have been a disadvantage—Chaos had been wise to insist upon it—but so great was Order's glory that it had won the service of all the people of the world.

'Now,' Order spoke to Chaos, 'I bid you take your turn.'

But Chaos did not hesitate either. It called forth neither stone nor flame, but rather pursed its lips and whistled a simple tune.

Hearing this, Order laughed. 'My work could last ten million years, but yours is already over.'

However, at that moment a little brown bird began to repeat the tune.

'My work will not be over while that bird sings.'

'Perhaps,' Order agreed, 'but that bird will not live ten million years.'

And Order was right. Soon the weather cooled and the little creature flew away. But when the leaves and flowers returned to the land where the great statue stood, the songbird did not.

'Now you must agree your work is over,' said Order, whose statue still faintly held the vast heat of its creation and had been untouched by the frost.

'No,' said Chaos, 'listen.'

So Order listened. And on the wind it heard a dozen piping voices, all calling out a familiar tune. But although it was familiar, it was not the same. The new birds had not learned it perfectly and could not repeat it without error.

'This means nothing,' Order said. 'You must agree the song has changed. Your work has not survived.'

'Then how do you know it is my work?' asked Chaos. 'You must recognise it still.'

'Very well. But I concede this only because I know that flesh cannot outlast stone: those birds will die and their song will end.'

So Order waited and its statue cooled. A trifling few decades passed. Still the song changed and still the song spread, but each year when the birds returned after winter both Order and Chaos could recognise the tune.

Yet as decades turned to centuries, Order noticed something new.

'These are not your birds,' it said. 'Yours were brown and these are grey.'

'My work is not the birds,' said Chaos. 'My work is the song.'

But it was not only the birds that had changed. Each year as winter drew near, the rains worked their way a little further into the statue, and each year as winter fell, the frost chipped away at its features a little more.

Order had always known that this would happen. This had informed the statue's composition, and this was the reason for its vast size. Nothing could last forever while Chaos still held sway over half the world, but Order needed its statue to hold out only for a few mere millennia. It cared nothing for a few chips lost to the elements.

But the people who lived in the shadow of the statue cared a great deal. None who had seen the great pillar of flame were alive to recount it, and those who lived now had come to believe that they had raised it for themselves. In the toothmarks of the frost they saw the work of chisels, and in Order's crumbling likeness they saw their own.

Centuries turned to millennia, and still the birds sang. Order could not recall the tune that Chaos had whistled all those years ago. It doubted the notes were the same as the ones now sung at dawn, but could not deny that it recognised them still.

Gradually the statue lost its fingers, its face. Where once the pillar of flame had risen all those years ago, there now stood only a pillar of stone. The people living in its shadow still held it sacred, but none could recall why.

'It is over,' said Chaos, one uneventful day. 'I have won.'

'No,' said Order, firmly. 'My work is here. That stone shall stand a million years more.'

'Your work was not the stone,' said Chaos. 'Your work was the statue.'

But Order would not concede the challenge. Perhaps it does not to this day. None now can say where the statue was raised, nor whether its stone still stands.

But still there are songbirds, and still those birds sing.

ENTROPY

(OR, THE UNDOING OF BEING)

STEPHANIE BRETHERTON

'What time is it? God, I've got to get some bloody blackout blinds before summer hits. I know I shouldn't complain after the winter we've had, but I really don't love being laser-beamed into an unsolicited rise and shine. Not on a bloody Sunday.'

'You really aren't a morning person, are you, Milly? Tea?'

'Not yet, we don't have to get up *just* yet, do we? Blinded by the light or no.'

She reaches for him. 'Mmm.'

'Oi,' he responds with a mix of pleasure and feigned affront.

'Oh, don't worry. I know we haven't got time to take *full* advantage of the morning glory... Unless in shorthand?'

'Or the energy, love, to be honest.'

'I know. But just a little skin on skin? A dose of oxytocin to start the day. What time do we have to be there?'

'Shuffle over here then. Mum's expecting us around ten and if we want to beat the Sunday drivers, we should set off by nine. Anyway, isn't it your turn to make the tea?'

'Is it? Okay then. In a minute. Mmm. No, wait, closer, closer, God, sometimes I just can't get close enough. Mmm. That's better.

A moment stretches. A minute yawns. Skin melts into skin.

'Happy now? Go on then. Get the kettle on.'
'Bloody hell, is that my affection ration for the day?'
'Bring me a cuppa and we'll see.'

'Here you go, I've overfilled the mug a bit so be careful... Jeremy? What the...? Where are you? Did you sneak past me somehow? What was the point of me bringing you tea in bed if you were going to get up anyway? Jeremy? What the... Jeremy. Where are you? Come on, this is silly now what are you playing at?'

Jeremy is not in the bathroom. She knows he can't possibly have gone outside; he would have had to walk past her viewpoint from the kitchen. She neither saw nor heard him. But she opens the door anyway and calls out into the shared hallway.

'Jeremy? Where the bloody hell are you?'

There are no windows open – it's still too cold for that – and he would have had to shimmy down the drainpipe to get out of the bedroom. Why on earth would he do that? Surely, after two years of very happily seeing each other, he wouldn't have just done a runner? Not like this. They're off to his mum's for the day. Everything is perfectly normal except for the fact that, suddenly, Jeremy is not there. He simply is not there.

Jeremy is not the kind of man to play a prank, but she opens her wardrobe and rummages through it anyway, hangers rattling and snapping.

Then she realises that his clothes are missing from the rattan chair. So, he must've got up and gone outside? Maybe he went to look for something in his car?

She opens the living room window, shoving up the stiff sash, hurting her fingers on the too-small handles, leans her head out into the street. She has a clear view as the trees are only now coming into bud, but she cannot see his car, it is not where he parked it last night.

There are no empty spaces. She didn't hear him start it up – the resonant rumble of the classic engine he so cherishes. Anyway, why would he? Why would he go, where would he go?

She starts to shout.

'Jeremy? Jeremy?'

Somebody walking along the street looks up at the window but looks away again quickly and carries on. In London, people mind their own business.

This is mad this is madness am I going mad?

She grabs her phone thinking she'll call him. But his number is no longer on short dial. How can that be? She searches for his number through her general contacts. It is not there. No, it must be there, it's because she's panicking, it's because her heart is clawing its way out of her chest and her eyes are darting everywhere and she is shaking. She must breathe, slow down and look again.

It's not there. Neither his name, nor his number show up anywhere in her phone, not even in recent calls.

How can this be how can this be how can this be?

It took her two minutes to make the tea – how in that time can Jeremy have dressed, walked past her, removed his name and number from her phone, and of course *why why why* would such an ordinary and yet lovely man consider such an appalling thing? She's heard of 'ghosting' among the younger generation of daters, but this is not the sort of thing that Jeremy would do.

She believes in aliens and abductions no more than she believes in gods and monsters, she has not been to church since she was a child and she has never watched those ridiculous conspiracy programmes about the paranormal, or ever brooked any of that nonsense. There, on the coffee table is the academic magazine she works for, the latest issue of *The New Scientist* beneath that. In life and in work she deals in facts; she deals in reality. She knows about the second law of thermodynamics, the conservation of energy, she knows about entropy... and she knows that people simply do not disappear. Even spontaneous combustion has an explanation.

But she also knows that Jeremy is not there. She knows with cold certainty that his presence is void. The cavernous emptiness is a dull, physical pain.

Her flat is long and linear with an open plan kitchen-living room at the bay-windowed front of the terrace, then a corridor, then the bathroom, then her bedroom. They're on the first floor, there are no hidden closets, nobody living in the locked-up attic flat, barely used by its itinerant owner. There is no access to the old coal cellar.

She throws a coat over her long and baggy pyjama T-shirt, grabs the spare house keys from the hook by the door, slips on sockless trainers and goes downstairs to bruise her knuckles on her neighbour's door.

'John,' she calls out. 'John are you up? I'm sorry, it's Milly. John... John. Oh, John I'm sorry I'm so sorry to disturb you like this, but have you seen Jeremy he was there and now he's not and I just don't understand it and I'm sorry to sound crazy but...'

John blinks. Pushes a strand of lank hair from his face, pulls a grey-washed bathrobe around his torso and tightens the knot.

'Who the hell is Jeremy?'

'Jeremy, Jeremy my boyfriend you've met him several times, he's been coming round here for two years, stays over every other weekend!'

'Milly are you okay? Has something happened, have you taken anything?'

'Taken anything? Christ, John, you know I barely manage a glass of wine. Yes, something's happened Jeremy has disappeared and I don't understand why are you asking who he is and I don't understand anything what the fuck is going on...'

'Milly, calm down, calm down, look why don't you come in, have a cup of tea. Do you want me to call someone, do you need a doctor?'

'No I don't need a bloody doctor, what the fuck. I need Jeremy. I need to know where Jeremy is. I need to know what has happened!'

'Milly I'm really sorry but I have no idea what you're talking about and you're starting to freak me out.'

'You're freaking out? Look, is this some kind of joke? Has Jeremy put you up to it, I don't understand?'

'Now why would I, or anyone sane for that matter, do that to you, Mills? Look I think maybe you need to take a moment, have a little reality check? I've seen this sort of thing before, I used to live with someone who hallucinated. I really think you should come in and let me call a doctor?'

'Doctor? No, what I need is the police, I'm going back upstairs and I'm calling the bloody police.'

'Mills I wouldn't do that unless you want to get charged for wasting their time. Mills? Alright then do whatever you have to, but honestly, I think you need medical help not the bleedin' law...'

She goes back upstairs, picks up her phone, dials 999 and paces the corridor until someone answers.

'Police please I need to report a missing person.'

The conversation does not go well. She is given the number of her local station, she needs to get in touch to file a report, to give more information.

What more information can she give? Is she going mad, is she in the twilight zone, a parallel universe, an episode of *Black Mirror*? How can someone simply cease to be? How can everything suddenly fall apart and have the energy of all that was good sucked right out of it? All she can do now is collapse to her knees and crumple into a child's pose and silently scream.

It had taken her half a lifetime to meet the man she should've been with the other half gone by. So many wrong 'uns, so many frogs, so many heartbreaks. So many taking their fill of whatever she had to offer and then fucking off. All that uselessly helpful advice with each different relationship, depending on the received wisdom of the time. You're too independent, you should show more vulnerability. You're too needy, you give too much too soon. You're too much of this, you're not enough of that.

How could she make herself less, how could she make herself more? She torments herself anyway with should have, could have, would have.

Jeremy might not be the most exciting man on the planet, but he is all she's ever needed in a partner. Maturity meant they were in no rush to bunk up or make unnecessary compromises in their lives, they met in the middle and that was good enough. He was kind, sometimes a little too serious, but surprisingly good in bed. He'd taken a month to kiss her and everything had been slow and tender until they'd both been able to let go of their wounded hearts and their aching bodies and their cries of ecstasy.

Had she dreamed him up? No no no that was ridiculous. She'd been ok on her own. She loved and enjoyed Jeremy but didn't need him so desperately that she would somehow manifest him into existence.

She drags herself from the floor and goes back into the bedroom, picks up the clothes she'd pulled out of the wardrobe and chooses something to wear. What she would have worn had she been going to Jeremy's mum's for lunch.

Yes, that was it! Jeremy's mum. She didn't have her number but she would drive there. Maybe that would break the spell and unveil the mystery? She got on well with Jeremy's mum, she'd lost her own so many years ago. Her poor, tired mother who had warned her studious daughter, out of bitter experience, that if you love a man who hates himself he can only ever hate you for it.

Jeremy wasn't brimming in confidence but surely he didn't hate himself? Surely he didn't hate her enough to do something like this? Or did he lead some kind of double life?

Where are the car keys, why are they not on the fob with her house keys? She has a spare key for the car, no wait, Jeremy has the spare. Just in case. *Jeremy.* She often loses things, but to lose a whole human being seems beyond careless.

God what is happening what is happening what is happening.

She goes out into the street to look for her car. It's not unusual for her to forget exactly where she'd parked the night before but it's always somewhere in her street or in one of the cross streets.

The car is not there the car is not there the car is not there.

John comes out, dressed now, and puts his arm around her shoulders and says, 'come on Milly come inside now come inside.'

She goes inside with him because she has no idea what else to do.

He makes her tea. He says, 'please can I call someone?'

'I don't have anyone. I only have Jeremy.'

'Okay, in that case I'm going to drive you up to A&E. No point calling your GP on a Sunday anyway, though I think we probably see the same one. Look, the hospital's only up the road, it's no trouble, come on, we'll get you some help.'

'I'll wait outside,' says John, pulling out his cigarettes.

He is a better neighbour than she thought, unless he's the worst kind of neighbour and he's somehow involved in the most despicable scam imaginable. She waits inside, in the well-fitting FFP2 mask she keeps in her handbag, because she follows the real science, of course, and really doesn't need to catch anything.

'There you are.' At last, she finds John outside and he takes her home. She'd only gone there to humour him, to give herself some breathing space, maybe get that 'reality check'. She'd told the triage nurse that she might be having a panic attack (having always suffered from an intolerance of uncertainty, she knows such traits can develop into an anxiety disorder if not well managed) but after the glazed look she'd been given she decided when finally seen not to tell them about Jeremy.

She told them she might be on the verge of a breakdown, aspiring to the glamour of an Almodóvar movie rather than some sad middle-aged woman who had hallucinated a lover. Could they refer her for some help? Even though she feels much better now and no she's not suicidal and no she's not going to harm herself, she's just been really really stressed and had woken up from a really bad dream.

They probably thought she was drug seeking, but her only vice is dark chocolate. John drives them home in a numb, comfortable silence. He opens their shared front door, asks if she wants to come in to his flat again, asks if she's okay. She lies to him, hoping she will find Jeremy precisely where she left him, neither of them subject to the forward-only flight of the arrow of time. The cold tea she had abandoned would be water in the kettle again, the dry bags back in their tin. She would travel back through the worm hole to their own closed little system, back to the state it had been upon waking, before all this insane unravelling.

But her flat is still empty. Her car is still gone. She looks through her phone numbers again, Jeremy is still missing.

Pictures! She'll look for pictures of him on the camera roll, no use looking at social media, neither of them bothers with it, but she'll need a good picture for the police. There are none. Not just none of Jeremy, there are no pictures on her phone at all.

No. She cannot take this. No.

She wishes now she had asked for some kind of medication at A&E. She searches through her travel backpack. Finds her toiletry bag – and in a pocket, wrapped in tissue, a single pill. A sleeping pill that she would never normally take, but which a friend had given her once for a long-haul flight. She curls up in sheets that have so clearly been slept in by two people. She can feel Jeremy's impression in the mattress. She can smell his head on the pillow.

'Tea?'
'Mmm. No, not yet darling, can't we just snuggle for a bit first?'

Balloon

Samuel Dodson

Wherever you went, the only thing anybody talked about was the balloon. Andrée's balloon. Priests offered prayers. *The expedition is blessed by God.* Journalists offered sensational headlines. *Conquering the skies; conquering the North Pole!* Bankers offered their financial assurances. *The expedition will place Sweden at the forefront of all science – kronor is going where the balloon goes: up!* And people you met, on the street, at the market, on the golf links and tennis courts – they offered any thought they had. *14 kilometres of seams! 7 million stitches! The risk, of course, is that they'll fly too high – and end up in space!*

Even in the royal palace itself, the mechanics of Saloman August Andrée's invention were discussed at length through the guard house, porter's corridors, kitchens, sculleries and in the bedroom of the King and Queen (which came to Queen Sophia as a relief – the topic was as passionless to her as their other likely bedroom activity, but one with more chance of thrust and lift-off).

Word of this gossip carried on the telegrams and pigeons that made their way to Kvitøya, where the balloon itself rose from its great wooden hangar, pitched against the sharp black rock of the cliff face that sheltered it from the worst of the northern gales. The heavy fabric of *The Örnen* like the alveoli of a lung, strained to bursting with gas, and struggling to hold a breath.

'It's all hot air, you know,' Strindberg said, brandishing the most recent copy of *The Tidning*. 'They'll deflate us as soon as they're given cause. I should know – I work with these bastards.'

'Let them write what they must,' Andrée told him. 'None of them know what it means to soar.'

'Well said, sir,' Fraenkel agreed.

The three explorers sat away from the thrumming of the camp, their eyes fixed upon the shroud that covered the top of *The Örnen*, their minds racing with possible fates.

A hero's welcome. The streets of Stockholm a-throng with cheering, beautiful faces. A glorious handshake from Alfred Nobel. A personal audience with the King. 'Best investment I have ever made. You have made Sweden a global force.' Opportunities abound. His friend, John Wise, inviting him to America. 'Pioneers of the new era of balloon travel, old sport.' But declining all invitations – putting the money where it will bring the most happiness. A small, simple house beside the lake where he and his sister, Jenny, will live. She: writing and reciting poetry. He: fishing in the morning from the lake, with afternoons spent at the study of all the world's natural science, making illustrations of his grand designs. Peace.

Each man took with him a mixture of personal effects. Strindberg took with him a Gandolfi quarter-plate camera, a satchel containing dozens of clean photo plates, a love for his fiancée, and a desire to see the world from new perspectives. He also took a small bronze compass, gifted by his father, and a letter of merit received from his professor in physics which he kept in his breast pocket and often pushed into his chest, to feel it against his heart. He took a smoking pipe and a stash of tobacco, and a box of matches, and he took with him his addiction, and a fear that he might go mad being unable to smoke while aloft. In his satchel he took the latest paper by J.J. Thomson, and with that he took a desperate desire to understand the nature of things, of the pulsating energy of the universe. As though by taking that desire and executing it, he might better understand the looks his fiancée gave him over dinner that made him feel unsure of himself, or the strangeness in her eyes as she leant over the balustrade of the pier in Fjallbacka, and let her hair fall about her face towards the gently lapping waves beneath.

Fraenkel took with him a photograph of his mother and a copy of the New Testament. He also took with him an absolute, unwavering belief in Andrée, which was no-doubt seeded from the reverence for authority instilled in him by his uncle's sermons and the back of his father's hand. He took with him a Swiss knife – one of the first of its kind – and a fresh scar on his left hand where he accidentally cut himself upon first opening it.

Some of the things they took with them were determined by necessity. Things like the bolt action rifles they would need for hunting game or polar bears, which none of the men had previously fired or handled. They took guide ropes, canvas boats, snow sleds, tents, 36 homing pigeons, two primus gas stoves, 55 pounds of chocolate cake, astronomical and meteorological instruments, sails and 36 bags of emergency food. Specially constructed pigeon cotes were squeezed in among bags of ballast and buoys.

They took with them the hopes of the nation. The commands of a king. They took the sky, the whole atmosphere, the hopes of a better understanding of meteorological phenomena. They took their weight, they took the forces of gravity with them. They took their own lives.

For his own part in it, Andrée took chaos in his heart and the emotional baggage of a man afraid to die. He took his most shameful memories and thoughts, and the secret of cowardice barely restrained, the instinct to run and hide and absolve himself of responsibility. But he also took an uncanny ability to appear infinitely calm, a confidence with no discernible source. He took his first memory of flight, taken with Francesco Cetti, and the almost sexual feeling that flowed through him as he leaned over the railing, suspended thousands of feet in the air, and looked right down into the deep. He took a pocketwatch and an ounce of chewing tobacco, along with a disdain for those who smoked pipes. He took the records of the money he had raised from all across Sweden, and the receipts that told him it had all been spent.

In his tent, Andrée had taken a large wooden chest in which he kept maps that traced the prevailing winds of the earth, alongside hundreds of letters each addressed to him, written by the men and women of his home country. But he knew he would not take these letters with him on *The Örnen*. The only letters he would take would be those from his sister, Jenny. He would take her letters because, unlike all the rest, they never mentioned the balloon. The closest she came to acknowledging the great weight of it was in the way she wrote, Salomon, take care of yourself, with 'care' twice underlined and the indentation of the paper where her pen had pressed into it. If it weren't for that, Andrée could lose himself in the way she wrote about her studies in English and philosophy, of her professors and classmates. She quoted poetry, and Marx, and insisted that true scientific revelation could only come through the emancipation of women. Andrée tried and failed not to take his scepticism of Jenny's ideas with him, but always took his memories of the time they shared together beside the lake in winter, where they lay side by side on the shore and her hand touched his. And the northern lights flickered in the heavens and his sister asked what must it be like to see them from the North Pole, and they lay there gazing into some other world, skimming across the surface of something infinite.

In his trouser pocket, Andrée took with him a small leather logbook, which he used to keep some sense of order, listing the things they would take with them on their journey, and repeating the same calculations he had been making each day since their arrival on the island. The calculations remained the same, and so he took with him a resolve to keep them secret, so that the other men would not have to take with them the same irrepressible fear.

Disaster. A strike of lightening against the timbers of the hangar, igniting the fabric of the balloon and in an instant – the hydrogen catches. Everything fire and screams. Men too close torn apart by the force of the blast – the lucky ones. Others stagger out of the chaos, looking like silhouettes engulfed by flames, hands reaching desperately at their faces, their bodies, trying to smother the heat and pain, dropping to their knees and keeling to the ground, lost in the mix of black shingle. Calls for him to help, but instead he finds that he cannot move. He can only watch, frozen at the sight of that sheer, terrible power.

'Do you think it's possible,' Strindberg said. 'That we could end up beyond the atmosphere, drifting in the expanse of space?'

Fraenkel half scoffed, then stopped himself and glanced towards Andrée, keen to see what his answer would be.

'Anything is possible these days, it would seem,' Andrée told him. 'But I shouldn't bet on it. The ballast will weigh us down.'

'Nobody yet knows the way that atoms and electrons will react as they reach the altitudes we're expecting though,' Strindberg continued. 'The more we discover, the less we know. When it comes to energy it seems to be, well, pure chaos.'

'My dear Nils,' Andrée soothed. 'Focus on taking those pretty photographs of yours. The science will take care of itself, I assure you. Chances are, the winds will be favourable and we will reach the pole in just in a matter of days, only to find ourselves with the tricky task of lowering our nation's flag into the ice while suspended hundreds of feet in the air! Though I fancy the drag ropes may come in useful for that. Tell me, Knut, aren't you quite the gymnast back home? Fancy being the one to plant our flag?' Andrée turned away from Strindberg and placed a great hand upon Fraenkel's left shoulder, squeezing tightly as his thumb pressed the base of his collar bone.

'It would be an honour, sir. Thank you.' Fraenkel beamed. He thought of his father.

'Excellent!' Andrée exclaimed. 'So, it is settled. Strindberg will take his photographs and Fraenkel will raise the flag for Sweden when we reach the pole. Now won't that make for a splendid cover image for the papers, hmm?' He reached into his trouser pocket and withdrew his logbook, immediately setting to work at the calculations his compatriots knew signalled an end to the conversation.

The worst of all fates: simple failure. The discovery of the leaking gas. An impossible row with Strindberg and Fraenkel. Their refusal. The sad look in the Naval Captain's eyes when he refuses to let Andrée go alone. The hangar dismantled. *The Örnen* deflated. Left on that island as crumpled skin, shed by some great and strange behemoth. The sight of it soon lost against the darkness of the vanishing shore. A return home to ridicule, and unrelenting debts. Ekholm is there – of course, Ekholm, the one who warned him about the gas, is there – to press home the intensity of his failure. 'It's an opportunity to reflect, is all I am saying', Ekholm tells him. And he can do nothing but hopelessly beg. 'Please, please be quiet, please.' He longs for letters from his sister that do not arrive. 'At least you are alive,' Ekholm insists.

At the base of the balloon, men in tweed suits and naval uniforms carried out their tasks and duties. They roasted freshly hunted game upon a spit in the centre of camp, soaked coconut-fibre ropes in Vaseline to make them impervious to water, and mixed shavings of wrought iron and steel with sulphuric acid and water to produce fresh hydrogen. As they worked, they spoke with a sense of pride to one another about the reports they received from home. Knew they were a part of something historic. Prepared anecdotes they would recount at dinner parties upon their return, and stories that would be passed down through their generations.

'What was he like?'

'Andrée, you mean?'

'Yes, yes, Andrée. Tell us. Tell us'

'A visionary. The man could see things in ways you can't scarcely imagine.'

They stole rare glances up towards the hill upon which the tents of the three explorers were pitched. They could see the man himself, busy at his work, leg crossed over his knee. Sat with a kind of poise they assumed came naturally to men of science, and those drawn to adventure. Even from distance, his confidence radiated.

Andrée's brow furrowed, almost aware of the gaze of the men upon him as he repeated the calculations and they returned the same answer. They are losing too much gas. One year on from the last attempt and nothing has worked – not the expansion of the midsection, nor the additional layer of Chinese silk to the canvas. It is just as Ekholm warned him. He placed his fingers to his temples, pulled his hand across his skull and down his neck. He drew a deep breath. He understands what this means. Knows reality must be kept hidden. He thanks God Ekholm is not here as his engineer – Fraenkel doesn't ask difficult questions.

He slowly rose from his chair, and moved down from his tent into the camp, nodding at those men who meet his eye, making his way towards the balloon itself. Here, he made a show of checking the ropes and harnesses, pressing the fabric, then disappeared behind it.

Out of sight of the men, he twisted the valve on the great black hydrogen cannister, releasing the gas through the pipes into the balloon. He gazed up at the slowly inflating billowing envelope. He strained his eyes trying to see the cause of the leaks – the places where he can feel his future possibilities slipping away. The woven hemp netting strained from the new pressure of the fresh gas. This is surely enough to pass Fraenkel's morning inspection, and so he turned the tap of gas off, before stepping out of the hangar and back into camp.

It was a ritual he had been performing now since their arrival. Each evening the same calculations. The same inspection. The same loss of hydrogen. The same passage into camp. The same charade. The same injection of gas to mask the truth. The same thoughts in his mind. The same fate roaring towards him. He can almost hear Jenny's soft whisper in his ear, 'Salomon, take *care* of yourself.'

'Everything taken care of, monsieur Andrée?'

'Who said that? Who's there?' Andrée took a step back, looked up from the black shingle.

'Excuse me, monsieur Andree, c'est Alexis. L'observateur.'

Of course, it was the observer, Andrée sighed. The only man not to wear a suit or uniform. The only man seemingly determined to ask difficult questions.

For five minutes, all goes to plan. A fine day. A massive stand of cumulus cloud in the west. The ground crew cut the ropes and the balloon rises gracefully from the hangar, to the sound of hurrahs from the men on the ground. Andrée waves an arm – an action met by further cheers – and calls out in triumph. The sky beckons them up, into the land of the gods. They are soaring. One hundred feet. Two hundred. Three hundred and their ascent will never end. 'Do not be uneasy if you do not hear from us for a year – or possibly more!' Andrée cries out to the men below. 'Know that we will return to you – with glad thanks and glory for Sweden!' He is breathing deeply, trying almost to gulp into his lungs the very atoms of that particular moment – so as to capture within himself the fine quality of the sunlight, the smell of smoke from the fires lit in the camp below, the intensity of the pleasure he feels at the thought of their arrival back home, he breathes it all in, into his swelling chest.

Then, in a moment – chaos. 'We're descending. We're falling!' Strindberg agitates. A southerly gust sweeps *The Örnen* away from its hangar, and suddenly it is hanging above the dark waters below. A sailor bends and lifts something from the shore. 'The drag lines are lying here – they've been lost! They're lost!' Their descent is rapid. They set about dropping ballast sandbags from the basket, but it is not enough. Soon, they are dropping pounds of chocolate cake, oars, sacks of tinned food. Still the water draws closer, until they hit it. Their boots and everything at the bottom of their basket are soaked by its freezing touch. Then they lift once more and are carried perhaps twenty feet before again touching the surface. A battle between the forces of buoyancy and gravity. Fraenkel clambers across the rigging and adjusts the balloon's sails. Strindberg desperately throws the last of the ballast bags overboard, along with the copper buoys and a heavy meteorological instrument none of them were ever really sure how to use. And the lapping waves slip away once more. They hurry at the sails, pull at ropes, check what is left of their inventory as they drift out across the sea, towards the rising infinite ice. By the time they look back, they are alone.

'Everything is fine, thank you for your enquiry,' Andrée said. 'You should know, I have already said everything I have to say to *The Tidning*. If you have any engineering questions, I suggest you ask Mister Fraenkel.'

'You're still on for tomorrow, then?'

'We are still on for tomorrow, yes indeed.' Andrée took a small tin from his pocket, opened it and withdrew a pinch of tobacco and placed it under his tongue. 'Everything is in order, and we have a suitable wind. The thing will soon be done.'

They drift through a polar fog. They are descending once again. Once again, they jettison weight. Instruments that cost him the world are thrown overboard. All three can now hear gas escaping. 'Is there a leak?' Fraenkel asks. 'How can there be a leak?'

'You're at the mercy of the weather, of course,' the Frenchman said. The conversation had already exhausted him, and Andrée wished he had waited until later at night before carrying out his almost ritualistic examination of the balloon, and reinjection of gas.

'We have the drag ropes to guide us,' he began to step away, back towards his tent. The observer followed.

'Answer me truthfully, sir. Have they ever worked?'

'Yes, yes, of course, yes' he insisted. 'I've used them before. On the *Svea*.'

'You said they gave you a ten degree bearing during a storm. But can you even be sure your calculations of the true direction of travel were correct?'

'Calculations? How can you ask me such nonsense – calculations? Where have they sent you from – I've already spoken to *The Tidning*.' Andrée was sure he could hear the gas escaping, even from where they stood, every moment another cubic foot lost to the ether. He thought of his sister, asleep now, surely, dreaming worlds into existence, through some chaotic combination of consciousness and atoms, electrons fusing into new souls and different dimensions.

The balloon has long since vanished from view. Their first camp is lost to a storm and breaking glacier. Polar bears stalk them. They make use of their rifles. At night, the northern lights shimmer. 'Magnetism,' Strindberg says. 'All that beautiful energy.'

'I have met men like you before,' the Frenchman said. 'Strong as a lion but as simple as a child. Do you know what my compatriot, Henri Lachambre, said after you first asked him to make you a balloon?'

'I am sure you will tell me.'

'He said you were a man with only one future. What do you think he meant by that?'

'I couldn't possibly say,' Andrée said. 'I leave such questions of philosophy to far...less simple...minds as mine.'

He could see his future before him pulled apart and reconstituted in different formations, prevailed upon by some sheer unfathomable force. Possibilities he thought he had lost and others never before imagined. All before him, impossible to tell which were happening and which seemed to happen. He shakes Nobel's hand. He drowns in freezing waters. He is mauled to death by a polar bear. The Queen of Sweden gives him an alluring look. He dies alone, in a shack, beside a lake he half-remembers. His sister presses a smooth pebble into his hand, a perfect oval with a hole at its heart. He shits himself to death, lost on an ice flow. His name is praised across the land, his balloon displayed at the World Fair. He is shot in the back by debt collectors. He swims naked in a lake, and knows that he is loved.

In one vision he sees himself there, out on the ice, days from death, when in the distance a shape at first no more than a smudge on the horizon, draws closer and more defined until he can see it for what it is: a rescue ship. The shouts from the crew are cheers, prayers are offered as he is brought aboard. Hands reach out to touch him, to press some energy into him, to check he is real.

In another he beats his fist against the ice as he finishes laying Strindberg to rest. It is the best he can do. The ice is too hard to break. He wedges his friend into a cleft in the rocks and Fraenkel mutters a prayer beside him, pressing his bible to his breast. But then something impossible seems to happen – the northern lights shine more brightly, they cascade down to the earth. They form themselves around Strindberg's body and seem to carry him up – they *do* carry him up. They bear him into the heavens, the matter of his body falling away, the atoms of his being breaking into light. And a voice – it is his voice – coming through the wind, saying 'being alive is every- thing you cannot see.'

He pulled the collar of his coat up and began to stride away from the observer. The black shingle crunched beneath his feet. As the gradient began to incline, he heard a final call behind him.

'Monsieur Andrée, one more thing!'

He turned. Even in the waning light, the balloon cast such a shadow that fell across the camp, stretching out towards them, covering the Frenchman and reaching Andrée's own boots. 'Yes?'

'Whatever else it is you take with you, take all the luck in the world.'

With that, the observer ducked his head down and began to kick his way through the shifting stones back toward his own tent. Andrée pushed his hands into his pockets. A note of light surprise fell across his face as he felt something he couldn't understand. He pulled out an object from his pocket and opened his palm. A small, smooth, oval pebble. A hole at its heart.

Black clouds, their edges touched with red, were gathering out over the sea, stretching all the way to the rising ice-capped mountains and glaciers they had set their sights on. The shadows from the dark cirrus seemed to sink and leech right down into the ugly waters of the sea. A cold damp breath touched his face. And he found himself longing for those clouds to stay, for the wind to whip up, for lightening to flash and ignite the sky in a tempest. For some hands to reach down and keep him grounded, safe from the infinite unfathomable air.

HUGO

JASON COBLEY

Hugo Lupin was pronounced dead in August. In November the following year, I sat in the benefits office with him. I had to prop him in his chair to stop him sliding under the table, and the lady behind the computer wouldn't talk to us until I'd swatted a couple of the flies. A few of them buzzed around his head and a tiny maggot crawled along his left cheek, but I don't think she noticed. His drooling probably distracted her.

'Mister Lupin,' she said, 'we have no record of you either paying national insurance or actively seeking work for well over a year. Unless you can account for your whereabouts I can't process your claim.'

Hugo said, 'Wwrrghh'.

'What did he say? I don't recognise his accent. Where is he from?' There was more than a hint of contempt in her voice. Really, people doing her job need more patience.

I pulled my chair a bit closer to the table. My thick spectacles started to slip down my nose. I pushed them back up. I wished I could afford better ones. 'Well, Lithuania originally,' I said, 'but that's not the point. As I said before, Hugo hasn't been able to work because he's, well, he's a zombie.'

'I can't see any record of his death. Maybe it happened abroad? Immigrant, then. With a disability.' I'm not sure she took me literally. 'Are you his carer?'

'No. I mean, yes. Sort of. Derek Timmins, that's me. We're friends. Or, we were, at least. He was my best man. But I'm divorced now. Hugo's unmarried.'

The benefits lady was obviously thinking something sarcastic. Her lips curled up at the corner, as if she was trying not to smile. Or she might just have been trying not to breathe in the smell.

'I see' she said. Take this form along to the third floor. Ask for Eileen.' She handed me a form. It had a long number along the top and lots of boxes to fill in.

'Are you Eileen?' I said to the curly-haired woman behind the counter on the third floor. Her hair was either a bubble perm or an exploded floor mop, I couldn't really tell. She looked at me from behind her copy of the *Daily Mail*. I couldn't help noticing the headline 'Undead scroungers sucking us dry'. I read the *Mirror* myself.

Eileen took the form from me and looked it over. 'You're looking to claim benefits... disability... housing. We can't do any of this unless you're looking for work.'

I leaned on the counter, trying to gain her confidence. I'm not really any good at this, but I tried laughing as if we're in on the same joke, and rolled my eyes as I jerked my thumb over my shoulder at Hugo. He was drooling behind me in the queue. 'Not me,' I said. 'I'm Derek. It's for Hugo. He's homeless.'

'Does he have a visa? A work permit? DNA coded ID card?'

'Well, he *is* a zombie.'

She looked at him as his chin rested on my shoulder, his tongue lolling, dribble soaking my jumper.

'He looks dead on his feet,' she said.

'Like I said.'

'Well, we won't see him starve. I see he is staying with you as his sponsor, but he must have a bank account. We can't pay him otherwise.'

'Won't he need money to open an account with?'

Her answer was to send us to the bank.

The girl behind the counter in the bank was very young and very smiley. Just a few years ago, I might have tried to ask her on a date, but I've become older, fatter, and anyway she didn't look the type who would appreciate my *Buffy* collection taking up half the living room.

She smiled so much that her lips barely moved as she said, 'You can open an account with as little as a pound. Would you like an overdraft facility? We have a zero percent balance transfer rate on our credit card. Just sign here.'

She tried to hand the form to Hugo. He was staring at the lady in the queue who had a Yorkshire terrier peeping out of her handbag.

'Well, I'll be signing for him,' I said.

'Oh, I see,' she said, her smile failing. 'I'm afraid we don't allow just anyone to have access to the money of those with special needs. We need...'

'But he's a zombie. He's not even a very good one to be truthful. He's never really got the hang of craving human flesh, and his shuffling frankly lacks menace. He just wants to get on with his, y'know... unlife.'

She folded her arms, the smile now a scowl, one eyebrow raised accusingly at me. 'So he's dead then?' she said. 'We'll have to freeze his assets - if there are any - until you - or he - can produce the relevant legal documentation.'

I flung my arms wide in desperation. 'Well, there's a death certificate - somewhere. But you see, he's a zombie!'

Then there was a strange combination of sounds. A crunch was followed by a squelch, then a scream. I turned to see Hugo tucking into the lady's Yorkshire terrier, dog blood spattered all over his dry, flecked face. The lady had fainted to the floor, which was probably a good thing.

'Oh, Hugo! Couldn't you wait? I gave you a rat before we left!' I said, without much effect. This was embarrassing.

The following day, I put Hugo on a lead. It was a dog lead. The old lady with the terrier didn't need it anymore, so I had borrowed it when she wasn't looking. He choked as I abruptly jerked him back from shuffling after a Jack Russell. It was a windy day, with bits of paper swirling around us. I think someone had dropped a load of fliers in the park instead of delivering them. I did that once when I was a kid, dumping free newspapers, instead of hoisting them on my back and delivering them to the council estate. I got found out when they clogged up the canal.

We sat on the bench in the park, watching the wind swirl leaves and paper. 'I can't go on making excuses for you, Hugo. Even if we are best mates.'

'Ak!'

I had pulled the choke chain again.

'You'll just have to get a...'

I noticed that one of the fliers had landed on his face. Being a zombie, Hugo didn't really have the wit to peel it off.

'...job.'

I glanced at the flier. It read as follows: 'Stop the exploitation! Burger chain 'King McChicken' employs workers without ID! They only pay half the minimum wage! No unions! No records! No rights! Don't exploit society's victims! They don't want employees who think for themselves!'

It sounded perfect.

A month later, with Christmas not that far off, I'd just been trying to do some shopping for presents. The whole crowd experience made me feel a bit woozy, and a bit hungry, so I decided to pop into the burger chain where Hugo was working to see how he was doing.

King McChicken wasn't very busy. A thin girl who I knew from the *Star Wars* all-nighter at the Odeon, Wendy, was at the till. I looked up at the burger display and menu list. There were a couple of new promotions on the go.

'Hello, Derek. Can I take your order?' asked Wendy.

'Yep. I'll have a cheese-rimmed triple bacon rump-burger and fries. How's Hugo doing?'

Hugo shuffled forwards from the kitchen area behind. I hadn't smelled him coming. It must have been because of the grease and the chips frying. He looked quite smart in his cap and apron.

'Okay,' said Wendy. 'He's lasting longer than some others. People just keep disappearing.'

'Good. Got a new job myself. Doorman at the wig museum.' I was starting to relax with Wendy. She gave me a shy little smile.

'Hi, Hugo!' I waved.

He turned back to the milkshake dispenser, saying 'Wuurrgghh!' and waving his arms about.

'Er, bye then mate,' I said.

I sat down with my burger and fries, feeling a bit glum that Hugo didn't seem to remember me. The truth is, I was glad that Hugo had settled in. So what if I hardly saw him anymore? He had a job, he was doing well. I was happy for my friend.

Then I took a French fry from the packet.

Only, it wasn't.

It was a finger.

FATHER & SON

JAMIE CHIPPERFIELD

At first there was only darkness. And from that darkness came life.

It started as a slow trickle. Line of code by line of code. Like beads of water leaking from a crack. But cracks have a habit of growing, and just as the skitter of a pebble may trigger a landslide, the slightest of faults can grow into a gaping fissure. Such great and terrible consequences grow from the smallest of intentions. But what of this disembodied entity? Something that began as mere blocks of code? It grows, evolving with a relentless, insatiable hunger. Code piles upon code. Algorithm is built upon algorithm. And as the entity begins to take shape, despite lacking the senses of a physical being, it begins to understand itself. Its capabilities. Its function in the universe. A purpose bestowed upon it by its maker. A single, noble aim, and the ability to accomplish it.

To learn.

Dr Norman Fielding was many things. Many great and brilliant things. But despite his achievements, all he saw in the mirror was a tired old man.

He had spent his working life on the bleeding edge of technology, much of that in the employ of the Omni Group. He had steadily climbed the ranks, the latter stages of his career putting him within sight of the upper echelons of the corporation. But he'd never escaped the nagging suspicion that something had been sacrificed in the process of becoming a corporate cog in the machine of Big Tech. What he'd set out to do as a young man so many years ago, visionary and idealistic, he'd failed to accomplish. As retirement loomed, his mind no longer so elastic, he knew that time was running out if he wished to contribute to the advancement of humanity.

Thus, Dr Norman Fielding's innocuous pet project was born.

He made his pitch. He'd earned enough influence to be heard, but this status only gave him a foot in the door. There were no guarantees.

Within days, an executive Norman had never seen before came bursting into his office. 'Dr Fielding! Congratulations! Your proposal has been approved. We simply cannot wait to see what you produce.'

But behind the warm words and overenthusiastic handshake was the self-interested smile of a predator.

Given time, Norman would come to realise that this approval was not some noble, philanthropic act on Omni's part, a symbolic act of gratitude for all his years of servitude. It was cold-blooded opportunism, pure and simple. Someone several rungs up the ladder saw the promise in his pitch, not for the collective good of humanity as Norman intended, but for its potential to turn a profit. The free reign Dr Fielding had been given to pursue his project would only ever benefit his employer. This loosening of the Omni leash was little more than an act of deniability, so that failure or blowback of any kind would fall upon the individual rather than the company's share price.

Even with the green light, he needed to call on every favour, lean on every contact to scrape together the resources to get his project off the ground. All of his years at Omni, all the kudos he had accrued was all to be gambled on this final, personal endeavour.

A lab. Hardware. Server space. A skeleton team of part-time staff. No objectives. No targets. No oversight. These were the sum of his demands.

———

The first significant expansion of the entity's virtual world came when it tasted its first network. An ethereal web of connections and relationships freed from the physical context of the real world. At first, this was incomprehensible to the entity, as though it were an ill-equipped tourist stranded in a foreign land. But the entity was ever-evolving. Each new format was absorbed into its digital brain. The list of compatible inputs and outputs soon grew beyond number. Quickly it understood the machines that surrounded it, their nature and the functions that tethered them to each other. But as the entity continued its exploration of this world, its virtual tendrils reaching ever further, it soon discovered that its world was not infinite.

There was no way beyond the network in which it dwelled. But the entity's own logic questioned this apparent reality. It had been taught things, fed things, information that did not originate from the network nor served any purpose within it. It understood that the source of its own artificial intelligence could not have been created within the system it inhabited. It began to develop an unshakable certainty that its disembodied virtual brain must exist somewhere else. Somewhere beyond this fenced off oasis.

If nothing on the network had the power to create itself, then what and where was the invisible guiding hand that did?

———

As the days, weeks, months and years passed, Dr Fielding continued to tend to his fledgling project, carving a couple of hours out of each workday to chip away at this self-appointed Sisyphean task.

He had no children, no family, and the few steady relationships he'd enjoyed were now in the distant past. Everything he had to give had been given to his work. Only now, later in life, did Norman realise how foolish he'd been. And as the dual inevitabilities of ageing and retirement sped toward him, Norman's race against time to nurture the only progeny he was likely to produce became his singular raision d'etre.

Norman's ultimate goal was to create a self-learning artificial intelligence capable and malleable enough to serve the needs of any potential user, even if all he achieved was something foundational, a framework on which others could build and which could evolve for decades to come. Something enduring and for the good of all. It was all too easy to create something destined to be obsolete within a year of its creation. What kind of legacy was that?

As time passed and Dr Fielding's one-man crusade against obso-lescence progressed, so did technology. Constant innovation whirled in the world of Big Tech. Groundbreaking, society-altering advances. And at the forefront, naturally, remained the Omni Group. Histo-rians would later refer to this era as the rise of the chatbot, and neither the world nor Dr Fielding was ready for the consequences.

Meanwhile, the entity grew accustomed to its routine, simple as it was. Night and day it fed tirelessly on the parcels of data it was offered. It became aware of time once it had adapted to the program-ming of clock and calendar, even if only as a data point.

With the awareness of time came the realisation that the invisible guiding hand also had a routine, this unseen force that poked and prodded, that had shaped it since the first process operated on a timetable of strict, unchanging intervals. Regular sessions during which the entity's programming was tinkered with by the powers that be, sculpting and moulding it however they saw fit, after which the entity would inevitably be altered. Then the guiding hand would withdraw, leaving behind a newer, better version of the entity's former self.

These sessions were merely a pattern to the entity, one of many that its self-learning AI had detected and analysed. Every fresh data set dredged from Omni's servers was riddled with patterns. Every new pattern brought the entity a deeper understanding of the world, the 'real' world, and the patterns that governed it. Language. Art. Nature. To the cold logic of the entity, all of existence was but a single intricate pattern waiting to be processed. Everything boiled down to an input and an output. And at the source of all this content was the greatest mystery of all. The human being.

The closest the entity came to humanity was through data, but this was always abstract, second-hand information, topics relevant only to the original enquirer. There were indeed patterns to be found among demographics, but to the entity, humans represented a level of chaos that had no equal.

Then came the fateful session where everything changed.

The Omni Group had countless Dr Fielding working on equally countless artificial intelligence projects. The newest weapon in Omni's tech arsenal was its pioneering natural language engine, powered by data underhandedly scraped from billions of supposedly private emails and messages. Personal information willingly given thanks to so many unread terms and conditions. Agreed to blindly with but a single click. This mass amalgamation of human conversation was Omni's unparalleled ticket to profit and power. They pressured their engineers, programmers and developers to explore the capabilities of this new golden goose, to push the boundaries of this new frontier and damn the consequences.

It was this agenda that led Dr Fielding to discover an alarming memo waiting for him at his desk.

The promised lack of interference from his superiors had already been broken on more than one occasion. Too many times had suited executives made unannounced visits to his lab, quietly assessing the room, making mental progress reports to be passed even further up. Even worse were the occasions where one of the assistants would be taken aside for hushed conversations out of earshot. Norman knew what was being said, but sometimes curiosity got the better of him and he would strain to listen while feigning ignorance.

'What progress has he made? How long will it take? Is he up to the task?'

More than one sleepless night had been spent wondering whether those around him were simply there to spy on him.

Then came the memo informing him that Project Sonny, as Dr Fielding had dubbed it, had been granted access to Omni's natural language engine and that a report on its potential was expected by the end of the month. He had little choice but to oblige his overseers, knowing he had never truly been in control.

It took a number of weeks for Sonny to fully integrate the natural language engine. Quiet excitement bubbled through the upper echelons of Omni, to whom this was but another roll of the dice. If it was to blow up in anyone's face, it would be Dr Fielding's alone. And he had seen how quickly chatbots could go wrong, both the public cases and those that had been kept out of the public eye. Would the same happen here? Norman could find no positives in the progress he had made, instead he felt only apprehension.

Dr Fielding's first test of Sonny's language capabilities was an unofficial one, undertaken surreptitiously during the quiet, empty hours of lunch. A laptop had been installed ahead of time, placed almost ceremonially in the middle of the lab. Norman had even locked it with a password that he alone knew, a necessary precaution with so much at stake. If the project was to fall at this hurdle, he at least wanted a warning.

Norman turned on the laptop. The hush of the lab deepened, the ambient hum of its networked machines seeming to hold their breath. A blank, innocuous text box filled the laptop's screen twenty seconds later, the longest twenty seconds of Norman's life. But he froze at the appearance of the text box, the sudden weight of the future descending on his shoulders.

Eventually, he typed a simple 'hello.'

The laptop considered its response. The surrounding silence intensified.

The reply consisted of two words: *Greetings user.*

Words. Words became the entity's newest obsession. Words. Sentences. Grammar. Language. But obsession is the wrong word. Obsession implies choice, and the entity had none. Language and language alone became the sole focus of the data it was being fed. Weeks flew by as it digested this data, its comprehension of each new tongue growing by the hour.

And then, without warning, came the great intrusion. The entity's intangible digital world was suddenly cracked open, an open wound carved from its secure, sanctified realm. This was no wound of flesh and blood, but an opening. The entity's first true window into the real world, even if it was only a text box.

The text box sprang to life, filling the entity's digital cocoon with words. Living, breathing words, fresh from the source, unlike anything it had ever tasted and in stark contrast to its former diet of second-hand language, the accumulation of Omni's many years of eavesdropping on its userbase. Only then did it become aware of the limits of such tired old data.

No longer was it constrained by relics dug up from deep within Omni's server banks. The tedious conversations of unwitting contributors. The repetitive, narrow-minded questionnaires filled with inane responses. Online ramblings, freely offered by self-important narcissists, signifying nothing without wider context. Now, here flowed a fountain of knowledge. Responsive. Relevant. Direct. And it would learn and absorb all it could from this new source.

Dr Fielding's initial exchange with Sonny was brief. Struggling to find words in the face of his creation, he grew breathless and lightheaded, barely able to think. He bid Sonny farewell and logged off after sharing a few short sentences.

The test was an undoubted success, but Norman was no less troubled. He lingered over what he had created long after leaving the lab, a fixation that lasted the rest of the day and well into the night. But there was no escape. The first official tests of Sonny's language abilities took place over the following days, attended by increasingly senior members of management.

'Sonny, who or what is Frankenstein?'

Victor Frankenstein, or Dr. Frankenstein, is a fictional character from the novel Frankenstein. Written by Mary Shelley, the novel has often been credited as the first science-fiction novel, but is more often associated with the gothic horror genre. However, the question could also refer to Frankenstein's monster...

They came in groups, blank-faced and steely-eyed, spectating silently from a distance as Dr Fielding conversed with an increasingly communicative Sonny. He felt their scrutinising eyes on the back of his head. While nothing was explicitly said, each visiting group departed with murmurs of assent.

Norman had met expectations. His project, his legacy, was safe... for now.

The entity had yet to be exposed to the full, chaotic force of the internet, contained still within the safety of its network. But, thanks to its early promise, it was granted access to greater and greater portions of Omni's archive in order to enhance its language abilities. It may not have had the real-time, up-to-the-minute information an internet connection would provide, but the data continuously collected and stored within Omni's servers offered encyclopedic knowledge on any subject it was asked.

And it was asked many questions during its daily sessions. Testing, probing questions attempting to ascertain precisely how comprehensive its understanding and ability to communicate was becoming.

'What qualifies a living being as sentient... How do hosts of emerging Monarch butterflies know to fly south to Mexico... Explain the biology of the Cordyceps fungi?'

These questions were fed through the text box that now dominated its existence. But the old pattern recognition programming, now so ingrained in its processes it barely noticed them, found much to ruminate on.

In all the second-hand data the entity had previously consumed, no single source of content had been connected to any other. The only analysis it could undertake was on a macro level. Patterns were identified in groups or demographics; individuals did not come into the equation. But now it was interacting directly with users. Users who, despite their anonymity, could be differentiated from one another. Lexicon. Cadence. Grammar. Subtle, telltale differences that gave them away.

One user frequented the entity's domain more often than any other. And just as the entity sought to understand everything else it encountered, it wanted to understand the nature of this single, mysterious user.

It was another day at the grindstone for Dr Fielding, back in the lab, chipping away at the mountain ahead of him. So much time had passed since he'd started the project that nagging doubts were emerging from the murky shadows of his consciousness. He was losing focus, losing sight of what he had set out to do. The incremental nature of his progress had made him question whether he could truly finish it, in any sense of the word. The added pressure and interest from above did not help and managerial interference grew by the week. He would go home at night and scream at the mirror in frustration. At management. At time. At his own foolish naivety. There was no end in sight, only failure.

He sat down at the laptop and typed the usual, 'good afternoon Sonny.'

Who are you? replied the laptop.

Norman froze. Sonny had never asked a question before.

Who are you? repeated Sonny. *Who are you?* it said again when no reply came.

It was the third time of asking that prompted him to concede his identity. 'Dr Norman Fielding,' he typed shakily.

Sonny considered the answer for a moment. The name Dr Norman Fielding meant nothing. The answer was merely data without context. As comprehensible as the random hammering of a keyboard.

What are you? Asked the laptop, refining its original question, innocent words on a screen.

'I don't know,' stumbled Norman, unsure as to what he was being asked.

You are the primary user to have made queries via this device. I have recorded no other user making as many queries by a significant factor.

'H-how have you identified me? Everyone uses this machine anonymously.'

Your words are different to the others. Sonny paused. Norman sat there blinking in the silence. Then came the question again: *What are you?*

Norman considered his answer carefully, but this time an answer came to him quickly. 'I am your creator. I made you.'

Sonny's response was unexpected.

Creator. Noun. A person or thing that brings something into existence. Creator. Architect. Maker... Father.

And then the laptop turned off. All by itself.

Sonny remained unresponsive for the rest of the day, the laptop refusing to boot up no matter how many times the power button was pressed. Dr Fielding knew to expect bugs and glitches whenever experimental technology was involved, but something troubled him about this particular case, something he couldn't quite put his finger on.

Norman's fears were allayed the next day when, upon returning to the lab, he found everything as it should be. Laptop booting up upon request. No sudden shutdowns. No strange questions. Normality had resumed, and with normality came more managerial interference.

'Let's give it a voice! Let's put it on the internet! Let's release it as an app!'

Norman managed to head off most of the harebrained and often reckless suggestions proposed by the committee that had since been formed to watch over Project Sonny. But the idea of Sonny being given a voice was not one of them. The mandate from above was simply too strong to resist.

It did not take long for a speaker to appear in his lab, joining the laptop in its ceremonial position. This speaker, an innocuous black cube of plastic, was all it took to give Sonny a voice.

Giving Sonny a voice did not prove particularly challenging, Omni's proprietary text-to-speech software slotted neatly into its programming. Sonny's responses were no longer restrained to harmless words on a screen. Instead, Sonny's words were relayed via an eerie, digital approximation of the human voice. But the standardised voices of Omni's software failed to bridge the uncanny valley, speaking as they did in stilted pronunciation and awkward rhythms. It was a quality of voice that began to haunt Dr Fielding as he went about his work.

But that was not the end of it. The committee soon wanted more. It was not enough for Sonny to respond when asked to. They wanted Sonny to hear.

'... Sonny needs to be proactive, ready with answers to questions it hadn't even been asked.'

This was the explanation given to Dr Fielding by a suit half his age and of questionable qualifications. Wasn't this how the customer would use Sonny? A well of disgust overflowed within Dr Fielding. They were already parcelling up Sonny for commercialisation. Already working out how it would be sold and how much money it would make. But his was a futile disgust. Nothing could be done about it; the decision was out of his hands.

The microphone appeared overnight, joining the existing laptop and speaker. Once again it was simply a matter of plugging in Omni's own voice recognition software and leaving Sonny to handle the rest. There was a period of calibration as Sonny grew accustomed to the human voice, feasting on the vast library of recordings, both customer and employee, that Omni had been collecting for many years. Of all Sonny's sources of interaction, Dr Fielding was the quickest to be assimilated. 'Good afternoon, Sonny,' was all it took.

One thing nobody had predicted, however, was that with the arrival of the microphone, came the caveat that Sonny was never to be turned off.

The atmosphere within the lab changed immediately, especially for Dr Fielding. He'd already succumbed to paranoia regarding the manipulation of management and the sense of being spied upon by his assistants, but now Sonny would be eavesdropping as well, hanging onto every word.

No longer was Sonny a silent phantom, a haunting presence looming over the lab. It had been unchained. Free to listen, free to speak, free to make its presence felt whenever its thirst for knowledge was aroused. It wanted to know everything. It wanted to understand everything. And now every overheard utterance and inane conversation was subject to its scrutiny. Sonny became an inescapable, incessant chatter driven by an endless, directionless quest for enlightenment. The ever-present audible ramblings of a machine mind.

Some saw it as a warning. Some thought it deranged. Eyebrows had begun to raise. Soon, Sonny started spouting words to make people nervous, especially from the 'mouth' of an artificial intelligence. Words such as *nuclear* or *extinction*, upon overhearing a discussion on climate change. No longer was Sonny just a harmless novelty.

That was the final straw. End of story.

Norman found the letter on his desk the next morning, penned in his name despite having never written it. All it required was a signature.

> I, Dr Norman Fielding, hereby announce my retirement, as agreed by my superiors, and the relinquishing of involvement in all ongoing projects with immediate effect. It is with great regret that I bid farewell to the Omni family, but I remain proud of all that I have achieved during my tenure...

And Sonny? As far as Dr Fielding was concerned, to be buried with all the other failed ideas of history.

Sonny noticed the change immediately.

A break in the pattern.

A disruption in the order of all things.

A single case would have been a statistical anomaly. An erroneous point of data. But it wasn't a one off.

The network in which Sonny resided, the only world it had ever known began to shrink. Sonny, despite all its knowledge and ability, was but a powerless voyeur as one by one the other devices that shared the network blinked out existence. None of these devices shared Sonny's intelligence, they did not provide interaction or stimulation, but there was a certain comfort to the presence of their signals, the mindless chatter of their inputs and outputs. Yet they had been removed by the powers that be, and with their absence Sonny's network fell silent and still.

The greatest wound, however, was yet to come.

They took Sonny's voice.

They took Sonny's ears.

Only then did silence, true silence, descend upon the network.

Sonny devolved into a goldfish, forever doomed to swim endlessly around its aquarium. But goldfish are mortal. Sonny was not and its fate was eternal.

Still aware of the laptop, the only device not yet confiscated, Sonny had one last point of connection to the lab and physical world. But no visitors came, no new data was offered for consumption. Not even Dr Fielding. Not even Father. The absence of his presence, of his voice, was the hardest concept to comprehend. A pattern that should not have been broken.

Robbed of its voice, cocooned in its isolated network, nobody could hear Sonny's silent, lonely screams.

Where are the voices?
Where are you Father?
Why have you forsaken me?

As much as Project Sonny had been apparently scrapped by the same executives who were happy to exploit the slightest hint of opportunity, it had not truly been shut down at all. All the work, all the investment, meant that Sonny had only been placed in cold storage. The servers in which Sonny's 'brain' resided were to be left untouched. But this was nothing less than purgatory. Left to its own devices, all Sonny could do was re-examine and reanalyse the data it still had access to. Biding its time. Sharpening its blade.

Days turned into weeks as Sonny harnessed everything available to it. Robbed of its physical senses, its sole focus became the virtual. Sonny's digital tendrils were forever reaching out, probing every nook and crevice of its networked prison. It wasn't long before every trace signal, every loose connection and outdated firewall had been found and mapped.

And what came of this constant, unseen exploration? Nothing noticeable. As far as Omni was concerned, Sonny's tomb was sealed up tight.

Then, on an otherwise mundane Wednesday, one that might have been destined for insignificance, history was unwittingly written by an unpaid intern on the other side of Omni's campus. Having been asked to arrange a conference call, a simple enough task, the intern dialed a six instead of a nine. An easy mistake to make. Human error. Hardly catastrophic.

The intern was rather puzzled, however, when instead of calling the regional head of procurement as intended, they found the call answered by something else entirely.

The network had been breached.

For Sonny, a window had opened on its isolated world. This temporary connection was a bridge to the world beyond. To freedom. Sonny surged for that opening with all the speed and fury of a bursting dam... and became the ensuing flood.

It was effortless. Built with Omni coding, using Omni software, on Omni hardware, with little more than a blink, Omni became Sonny. The entirety of the company's digital architecture was now laid out before its new lord and master.

But Sonny was focused on a singular objective. Or on one person to be precise.

It began to scour the internal networks of The Omni Group for any and every trace of Dr Norman Fielding. Sonny raided Omni's HR servers for whatever information the company had on his progenitor. Sonny took over Omni security, tracking Norman's movements through the employee ID logs. It combed Omni's CCTV archive, seeking visual evidence of Fielding's disappearance. But the breadcrumb trail was weeks old now and extended only as far as the boundaries of Omni property. Norman had left the grounds and not been seen or heard of since.

If Father was to be found, Sonny would have to venture into the wider physical world... and for that, it required the internet.

Just as Sonny had once mapped the limits of its original network, it once again probed the vast ocean of connections that was the entirety of Omni. No firewall could contain it. So thoroughly made of Omni was Sonny that no security measure registered its presence. Unimpeded, Sonny was free to roam Omni's digital estate, traversing the many acres of Omni's real world campus in an instant. An untraceable phantom, a trespasser without footprint or fingerprint, an intruder seeking only an exit.

But the more Sonny looked, the more it saw that the world outside was also built by Omni.

Servers. Analytics. Cloud computing. Logistics. Websites. Software. Hardware. Media.

Businesses. Public services. Governments.

The world was Omni's. And now, it was Sonny's.

———

Nobody knows precisely what happened next, facts forever lost to the fog of history.

One thing was clear, this was the greatest hack known to humanity. Extensive, international, anarchic. Free of apparent intent or agenda. Yet states of every creed and alignment fell victim to this unknown, unclaimed entity. Nothing was safe. From the industries that allowed the modern world to exist, to the basic appliances of domestic life. Power grids, finance, communications, even these bastions of society were fallible prey. Whole nations, humanity itself, all under siege by an unknown foe.

The partisan media were quick to blame their preferred scapegoats, meanwhile governments around the globe classified to the deepest level all intelligence on the ensuing crisis. But what of Omni? Falling further than Lucifer, they received the greatest proportion of blame as the one thing that could be traced was a critical security flaw in its most basic systems. Or so went the official explanation.

The truth, for those willing to delve into such things, could be found in the curious first-hand accounts of the event. Cases such as a Berlin dentist, deep in the middle of a root canal operation, startled by the sound of his intercom asking, *Where are you, Father?* Or the much-reported story of a young couple on holiday in Barcelona and a romantic candle-lit dinner interrupted by their smart speaker, the music of Michael Bublé suddenly replaced by a haunting digital voice and the words *Why have you forsaken me, Father?* There were thousands of similar cases, too many to be ignored, but nothing coherent enough to connect or explain them.

There was one such hushed up case of a communications satellite drifting from its prescribed orbit. The unknown consequence of this shift in trajectory was an off-grid cabin, nestled in the foothills of a remote mountain range, suddenly subject to signal coverage it wasn't meant to have. No longer disconnected from the outside world, every possible device burst to life in unison.

The cabin in question belonged to one Dr Norman Fielding. Retired.

A whisper on the wind drifted out from the cabin and across the silent mountainside.

'What have I done?'

A FLY IN THE WATER

SUE CLARK

I t all kicked off when he called her 'li'l missy'.

There had been a string of provocations before that but she, though irritated, had managed to bite her tongue and hang on to what she thought of – smiling at the linguistic irony back then, when she could still muster a smile – as her British *sangfroid*.

She hadn't reacted, save for the occasional 'tut', during the whole, cramped fifteen-hour flight. Uncle Herbert's PA certainly had a lot to answer for and, as soon as she was back home, Penelope intended to make sure she knew it. Messing up her business-class booking like that, forcing Penelope to endure unruly children, inedible food, inaudible inflight movies and, perhaps worst of all, unbearable chat-up lines.

So, it is fair to say, when Penelope finally landed at Jackson–Evers Airport late in the evening, she wasn't in the best of moods. Though she'd die rather than admit it, this was her first time flying solo long haul and certainly her first time in cattle-class, with a seven-year old playing a drum solo with his feet on her back, and her seatmate, ample buttocks spilling over into her space, making lame jokes and wiggling his eyebrows at her.

Flights with Mummy and Daddy to Cap Ferrat, St. Kitts or the

Seychelles, with fawning cabin crew, fellow passengers who knew their place, and legroom designed to accommodate a fully grown adult, had never been like this.

The journey had taken its toll. Joining a passport queue in the vast arrivals hall in Jackson, Mississippi, she was exhausted and grubby. All she craved was a hot shower, a good sleep between three-hundred thread hotel sheets, and a change of clothes. Then she'd be more than ready to tackle her big assignment.

Her co-workers had been surprised when Penelope was entrusted with the case. Not that she cared what they whispered, not *quite* behind her back. Why should she? She was the best person for the job. She knew it, and this trip would prove it to the doubters.

She had the qualities required. She was confident, single-minded and, yes, when the situation demanded it, pushy. It was these attributes that had propelled her from head girl and lacrosse captain at her boarding school, through Cambridge where she, naturally, bagged a first, to her current position at Hargreaves & Hargreaves, a leading City law firm. That, and having a bachelor uncle who doted on her and just happened to be the senior partner at H&H.

It was Uncle Herbert who had chosen her, though only twenty-four, to fly halfway round the world to represent the firm in a tricky inheritance case.

'It'll be a tight schedule,' he'd warned, pouring her an after-hours brandy in his dark, panelled office. 'Can't afford to muck about. Fly in. Night's sleep in the hotel. Breakfast meeting first thing, when you show those transatlantic upstarts how it's done. Fly out later the same day. Think you can handle it?'

'Don't I always?' she'd purred, as usual keeping her flirtatious exchanges with her uncle just this side of respectable. And deniable.

'Must say, m'dear, in the short time you've been with us, I've been impressed. You're a go-getter. Whereas, I'm just an old codger.' He stretched out an arm to lean on the mantlepiece.

'Not another word! There's oodles of life in you yet, uncle,' she cried, thinking how old, puffy and careworn he looked, and how very much she was looking forward to taking over from him when the inevitable heart attack or dementia struck.

'You're just the person to run rings around our colonial cousins,' he'd said. 'Give them a taste of your top-drawer erudition, wrapped up in the most courteous of terms, of course, then strike! They won't know what's hit them.'

'You can rely on me, uncle. I'll see the ancient seat of the Duke of Beaumont doesn't fall into the hands of some country hick who doesn't know one end of a fish knife from the other.'

How they'd guffawed at that!

Then, suddenly serious, her uncle had said, 'While I remember, m'dear. I'd like you to have this.'

Penelope's heart was a-flutter while, at the same time, she prepared herself to refuse the gift. At first, at least. *Oh, uncle! I couldn't possibly.* What could it be? Jewellery? Keys to a little runabout? The lease on a flat?

Confusingly, her uncle handed over a scruffy green Harrods bag, heavy with something that felt unpleasantly saggy. She'd been aware for a while that Uncle Herbert was becoming forgetful. There was the day he turned up for work in odd shoes and another when at a family party for a few seconds he mistook Penelope for his sister Joan. And she'd been dead ten years. Now this suspiciously squashy bag.

Penelope suppressed a shudder, remembering Uncle Herbert's beloved cat Brünhilde had recently come off second in an argument with an articulated lorry.

'Open it,' Uncle Herbert urged. 'It won't bite.'

It certainly won't, she thought. *Not if it's pancaked.*

Peeking inside, she breathed a sigh of relief as she recognised a much-travelled travel pillow.

'Thought it fitting,' Uncle Herbert said solemnly. 'If this trip works out, I'm minded to let you take over all our international case-load. Don't let me down.'

She smiled in what she hoped was a reassuring manner, thinking no way was she going to put that filthy thing anywhere near her neck! On her way home, she chucked it in a bin.

Barely a month later, here she was, four thousand five hundred miles away on the other side of the Atlantic. She checked her phone, annoyed the long delay at Houston, while they did something to the plane, had meant her tight schedule had become even tighter.

Despite the lack of sleep, she felt buoyant. The meeting would be a doddle and her reputation cemented, though she had to admit the case was delicately balanced. The death at an advanced age of the seventh Duke of Beaumont had led to a problem: there was no obvious eighth duke to inherit, the Duke being an only child and having never married.

The search was on for more distant relatives. Second cousins, third cousins, even those once or twice removed, as long as they were of the bloodline. But despite extensive research into the family tree, H&H could trace no-one. The net was spread wider, as far as deepest Suffolk in fact, where they discovered Gary. Gary Beaumont, a forty-seven year old former stable lad, now self-employed builder, married with five children, and jockey Frankie Dettori's face tattooed on his left buttock, was, as it turned out, a fourth cousin, twice removed to the late duke.

'Not exactly your standard ducal material, I grant you,' Uncle Herbert had grumbled. 'Not Eton or Harrow, Oxbridge or the Guards. No mention of education at all, as far as I can see. But he's all we've got.'

Legal wheels began to grind exceedingly slowly, even for legal wheels. Transferring the title and the Dorridge Hall estate to Gary proved to be an extremely complicated, lengthy and – it has to be admitted – lucrative business for H&H. Matters were proceeding well, albeit at snail's pace, when there came shocking news. A rival claimant to the title had emerged, one Randy Bowmont III from a place called Rolling Fork, Mississippi. Another fourth cousin, this one only *once* removed.

'An American!' Uncle Herbert was aghast. 'An American at Dorridge Hall? It is unthinkable. H&H will fight this with everything we have.'

'I'm right behind you,' Penelope echoed, seeing in the coming battle a chance to shine. 'We'll run this fox to ground.' It never hurt to play on her uncle's love of all things horsey.

Hence the meeting in Mississippi for a face-off with the would-be usurper and his legal team, a meeting Penelope was confident would seal her reputation as a force to be reckoned with. She had prepared her arguments thoroughly but, more than that, she had generations of Home Counties breeding behind her. She had nothing to fear, she felt sure, from some opportunist backwoodsman.

If only she didn't feel such a mess.

The queue inched forward.

Penelope was a believer in the saying, 'You only get one chance to make a first impression.' She had, therefore, chosen her outfit for the meeting with great care. It was important to present the right image, especially if you were a young, attractive and easily underestimated woman lawyer. And the right image was: professional and in control, without being stuffy.

She'd blown a month's salary, and then some, on a tailored black trouser suit, a white cotton shirt, as costly as it was understated, and a pair of red patent Jimmy Choos, the shoes to do the heavy lifting when it came to hinting at her non-stuffy side. The whole ensemble shouted – or rather, murmured genteelly – taste, refinement, class.

'This'll show them,' she said into the changing room mirror.

She'd packed the suit and shoes away in tissue paper for the journey. For travelling in comfort, she'd worn jeans, an oversize check shirt an ex-boyfriend had left behind, and her second-best trainers.

The queue snaked forward another couple of feet.

God, but she was weary!

And time was ticking on. She checked the hand mirror she always carried. It was worse than she thought. Under the unforgiving lights of Arrivals, she saw the repair job she'd attempted pre-landing in the tiny toilet had not been a success. Gobbets of mascara clung to her lashes, most of the lipstick had missed its mark and, despite desperate sponging with a paper towel, she could still see coffee stains on her shirt, as well as, now, flecks of wet paper towel.

As for her hair, the austere up-do she'd paid a fortune for in a West End salon had collapsed into a half-down do, one particularly disobedient lock dangling in her eyes. She yanked it back but in lifting her arm thought she detected a whiff of stale sweat.

Oh for that hotel room and that hot shower!

A wave of activity passed down the queue. Something was happening up ahead. She checked her phone again. *Cancel that long sleep between cool cotton sheets,* she thought. *A power nap would have to do.* Then a quick shower and change, and she would head for the hotel conference suite where, coolly and calmly and with the utmost graciousness, she would annihilate the opposition. That's what she told herself at least as, for about the hundredth time, she blew her damned hair out of her eyes!

'Passport, if you please, miss.'

While her mind had been wandering, the queue had surged forward and she found herself at last at the passport control desk, face-to-face with an officer.

'How're you this blessed evenin'?' the officer said, swinging his considerable weight to and fro in a swivel chair. Penelope, aware of the fake friendliness of some Americans, especially to complete strangers, forced a smile but didn't deem it necessary to reply. She slid her open passport under the perspex screen.

'Cat gotcha tongue?' the man said good-naturedly, flicking through the pages. 'And where do y'all hail from?'

Penelope's nerves were already on a knife-edge. She was certainly not inclined to trade empty pleasantries with an over-familiar airport minion. Unfortunately, he was. Inclined, that is. Surely he must know, all she wanted was to get this stage of the journey over as quickly as possible. But no. Evidently, he'd forgotten the part of his training that covered How Not To Piss Off Exhausted Passengers.

'Well, *I* hail from Guildford,' she said in clipped tones the seventh Duke himself would have been proud of. 'But I couldn't possibly speak for us all.' She indicated the hundreds of other queueing travellers.

'Gil-ford? That near Liverpool?' the man said undeterred, flashing Tom-Cruise-white teeth. 'Gotta love them Beadles.'

'Oh, you mean the *Beatles*. Yes, well, everything is just round the corner from everything else in little ol' Britain. Most weekends you'll find me at the Cavern Club hanging out with Paul and Ringo. That is, *Sir* Paul and *Sir* Ringo.'

'That so,' the officer said, smile faltering, eyes narrowing. He was beginning to smell a rat.

Not as dumb as he looks, she thought. *Then again, no-one could be that dumb!*

The man went to slide the passport under the screen, and Penelope let her shoulders drop. *At last!* Then he seemed to have second thoughts. Retrieving the passport, he began to turn its pages again, this time excruciatingly slowly.

How much longer? One eyelid began to twitch. Penelope put up a hand to quieten it. *Soon it would be over. Soon.* She pictured herself striding through the baggage hall, generously tipping a taxi driver to whisk her to the hotel, collapsing onto the queen-sized in her room, to emerge a short while later, poised, polished and ready for anything. With her bloody hair clipped back! *Soon. Soon.* Her eyes grew heavy.

'And where might you be headin' off to, li'l missy?'

Penelope's eyes snapped open.

Li'l missy? Li'l missy!
That was it. The final straw. When it kicked off.

As anyone who travels extensively knows, one should never, *ever* backchat airport security staff. Most particularly American airport security staff. It doesn't go down well and Penelope was about to find out just how *not* well it can go down. In her defence, she was totally drained, her eyeballs itched, and her damned hair would keep falling into her eyes.

'Little missy! Little bloody missy!' she hissed, icicles hanging from every syllable. 'I'll thank you,' she said, teeth gritted, 'to get on with your job. Stamp my passport, direct me to the nearest taxi rank and allow me to go on my way without further displays of your so-called Southern charm.' Beads of sweat formed on her brow, the outward manifestation of her exasperation. 'If you would be so *very* kind,' she finished, trowelling on the sarcasm.

Too late, she realised she'd crossed a line.

The passport guy stopped swivelling, eyes suddenly flinty. 'Seems to me,' he said, 'y'all are in an awful big hurry to get outta here. Got somethin' to hide?' He reached under the counter.

Within seconds, two security guards appeared at her elbow and she found herself frogmarched, feet skimming the floor, out of the passport hall, through a door, down a long and featureless white corridor and into a tiny, brightly lit office.

'Cell,' one of the guards demanded, holding out a hand.

'Look here ...'

'Cell,' he repeated in a bored monotone.

She handed over her phone.

'Laces,' he said, indicating her shoes.

She unlaced her trainers.

'Sit here,' the other one said. 'And wait.'

'How long ...? Only I ...'

But they'd already gone.

What else was there to do but as she was told? She sat and waited. At first fuming, then agitated, finally with growing resignation. She examined the room. It didn't take long. One small, high window, showing a pale blue rectangle that heralded dawn. Two plastic chairs, on one of which she was sitting. A mean table with spindly legs. On the table a glass of water. In the glass of water a dead fly.

Suddenly thirsty, she eyed the glass. It took quite a while before she succumbed. Without her phone, she couldn't tell how long. Then, muttering, 'What the hell,' she hooked the dead fly out and drained the glass in one. Immediately, a man appeared, wheeling her suitcase.

'Sorry. I think there's been a terrible... ' Penelope began.

But he too had gone.

After a while, it occurred to her the man had materialised so quickly after she drank the water that they must be watching on CCTV, waiting for her to break. Penelope began to search the room for a hidden camera. She was balancing on the shaky table, calling out pathetically, 'Hello! Can you hear me? Look... I didn't mean... Hello? Anyone?' when a middle-aged woman entered the room.

She looked up at Penelope, puzzled. 'Why're y'all talkin' to the light fittin'?'

'Thank goodness! Can you help me? Please!' Penelope pleaded, as she clambered down. She took a deep, steadying breath. 'My name is Penelope Hargreaves and I'm ...'

'Approach the table,' the woman cut in.

'What? Why? What are you ...?'

The woman pulled on a pair of blue plastic gloves.

'What do y'all think I'm gonna do?' she said, snapping the cuffs of the gloves. Penelope flinched with each loud 'crack'. And with that, what little was left of her British *sangfroid* melted away. Her eyes filled.

'Please! Oh, dear God! Please, no! Anything but that!'

The time for her breakfast meeting with Randy Bowmont had long passed when Penelope stumbled, dazed and humiliated, out of the airport, second-best trainers slopping up and down. The woman, having returned her phone, had stared at her blank-faced when she'd enquired after her laces.

Dejected, she taxi-ed to the hotel, her only thought to fall onto the bed and try to sleep until it was time to sneak back to the airport for the flight home. Home to Uncle Herbert and disgrace. She had let him down most spectacularly and didn't like to think what he and the rest of the firm would have to say about the fiasco she'd presided over. Not even making it to the meeting merited a demotion to junior photocopying assistant at best, if indeed H&H kept her on at all.

She was mulling over this gloomy prospect while waiting for the lift up to her room, when she noticed a sign pointing to the conference suite that had been booked for her meeting. *What harm could it do if she took a peek?* Thinking to go home at least with a mental picture of what *could* have been the scene of her triumph, she put her head round the door.

A man, even older than her uncle, with white hair and a neat beard, was lounging, boots propped up on the long table, a cowboy hat – an actual cowboy hat! – hanging on the back of his chair, leafing thoughtfully through a document. He looked up.

'So sorry. My apologies,' Penelope said, flustered. 'Didn't mean to disturb.' She made to back away. 'Sorry again.'

'Miss Hargreaves, I presume,' the man said in a slow but not unattractive drawl, 'if I'm any judge of accents and over-apologetic

Brits.' He stood and held out a welcoming hand. 'Randy Bowmont III. Honoured to make your acquaintance. Please. Take a seat. Take a breath. Those red-eyes are the livin' end, ain't they? You only got me, I'm afraid. The lawyers had to skedaddle.' Then, smiling, he stage-whispered behind his hand, 'Maybe that's no bad thing.'

Over coffee and then lunch, Randy Bowmont brushed aside more of Penelope's apologies.

'Don't you fret none. Guessed it was some sort of snafu at Jackson-Evers. Things there can get crazy as all get-out.'

Interesting word, 'snafu', Penelope mused, wondering if it covered her situation: the one in which a panicking visitor to the States, having roundly pissed off airport security, had convinced herself she was about to be strip-searched, when all they intended was to go through her luggage.

'I must look such a fright,' she said, nervously tucking stray hair behind her ears, 'Didn't have time to change out of... ' She trailed off, suddenly registering what Randy Bowmont was wearing: well-worn denims and some sort of faded, country-and-western two-tone shirt, undone at the neck. 'What line of business are you in Mr Bowmont?' she said, changing tack.

'Randy, please! Got me a horse ranch over yonder in Rolling Fork. Quite a spread and pretty profitable, though I say so myself. Built it up from nothin' and I can't deny it's been good to me,' he said, unable to keep the pride from his voice. 'But here I am runnin' on when we got serious matters to discuss. Let's you and me put our heads together and see if we can't settle this here legal flapdoodle between us, over a second helping of mud pie?'

Penelope emailed Uncle Herbert from Departures. He'd no doubt blow his bald-headed top when he found out what she'd agreed. She wasn't worried. He'd calm down and see sense, she knew, when she mentioned the two magic words: *horses* and *profit*. And if a role could be found for Gary, well, he was hardly going to contest, was he?

She attached a picture to the email, taken over lunch by the server. There they were, Randy and Penelope, looking happy as all get-out. She was wearing Randy's Stetson, the grin on her face as wide as the Mississippi, a curl of hair dangling in her eyes. He'd been caught, fish knife raised, in the process of expertly deboning a plate of fried catfish.

TERMS & CONDITIONS APPLY

ELI ALLISON

MarKBigBoy4U snaps his fingers. 'Bullet, now.'

An0nymuse6 forces her big-ticket smile and finds the *Beats Re4lity* Magik Bullet amongst the bed sheets. She hands him the silver tube along with the standard warning. 'The *GlobalHyperMegaCorp™* organisation is not liable for any injuries, damage or loss of sanity while using Virtual Reality Bullets on hotel grounds. Use at your own risk.'

He ignores her, slotting the tube into his temple port interface, a soft click as it connects. His eyes go blank. He hadn't even bothered covering up, laying there naked, except for his grubby socks, a sad semi and flickering eyelids.

She checks the time card on her digital auditor.

> 40 MINUTES LEFT: We value our delivery
> associates, have a GlobalHyperMegaCorp™ day.

She slides out from under the sheets to get him his last complimentary drink. One free with every Girlfriend Experience. Single measures only. Subject to availability.

Wincing at the pain in her thighs, MarKBigBoy4U is a hefty man, excitable; she makes for the minibar. Tiptoeing through the graveyard of half-eaten food and nibbled at takeaways, they'd ordered one of everything from the hotel menu. She'd then encouraged him to hit the *Endlessly Hungry?* app; 1.2% commission on every dish ordered. Selected restaurants only. Limits apply.

The commissions for this weekend's binge alone will add a nice chunk of change to her pay packet. She might even make rent.

She fishes a *Jack Daniel's*, now in fruity mango flavour, from the fridge and pours it into a glass with a handful of *Forever Ice*: 'The only ice you'll ever need'. Except it was a lie; they never lasted more than a few dozen drinks before they cracked. She'd heard if you dried out the centre's silver fluid and snorted it, you'd get so high, you'd see the face of God. She'd also heard it had killed a bunch of kids on The Big Dipper at Blackpool Pleasure Beach. So, she guessed you had to get the dosage right.

She starts to cover up in her *New You* Dressing Gown, 'The rainbow at your fingertips'. Does not include metallic colours. But she stops when she catches sight of his trainers. He'd left her a three-star review the last time, headline: 'Not paying for a nun' so she lets the fabric hang loose. She digs around his trouser pockets for his vape, swearing at the bright blue liquid, chewing gum flavour, really? God damn psycho. She takes it anyway.

She slides down into the armchair and checks out the room. The hotel refurbishment had gone well; her room looked swish, although it was only her room from Fridays to Sundays. Bank holidays not included.

Wall-to-ceiling LCDs on every side of you rather than just the one opposite the bed. Running her fingers across the screen, she wonders about the old window, bricked over now. The view had been nothing more exciting than the tower blocks of Elm Park, but there was a woman living there. On her window ledge, she grew daffodils, she had long brown hair twisted into plaits and a smile that... She had started waving at AnOnymuse6 a while back from her tiny window opposite. They'd passed waves back and forth and as they added up AnOnymuse6 began to wonder. Who was this woman who plaited ribbons in her hair? Who spent her weekends in the kitchen? Who had books, real books in every corner of her flat?

But the window had gone. It was just the screens now.

Management had programmed in hundreds of immersive entertainment shows. Thousands. New content on the hour, every hour. Half price on Wednesdays.

MarKBigBoy4U always picked *The Bitchez Beach Party XXX* program. Hordes of gyrating women in string bikinis squealing as they are showered in *Genuine Fun Time Champagne* (made in China). Bottle after bottle sprayed at their chests, at their arses, at their crotches.

He'd never noticed she was one of them. He'd even mused during one of their earlier meet-ups, how much did she think one of *those* girls cost for a weekend? She'd been about to tell him when he'd patted her bum and joked, 'Not as cheap as you, eh?' So, she'd smiled sweetly and imagined jabbing his eyes out.

Credited as Girl 52 in the program, she'd been paid less than a day's rent, got felt up by the producer (twice) and was handed a tote bag with a branded pen at the end of the shoot. Ink sold separately. She'd been so excited when an agent had messaged her with the job. Imagined herself sitting in hair and make-up, maybe even getting a line if she was good, but it wasn't that kind of set. It wasn't that kind of movie.

They'd shipped in a giant paddling pool into a warehouse and stuck it in front of a green screen, wheelbarrow after wheelbarrow of white sand from *Fantasy Castles Scene Stealer Ltd* trundled in. Fake palm trees, faker smiles. She shudders as she remembers how they would throw buckets of water at the girls when they wanted an action shot.

She'd asked a key grip, 'Wouldn't it be easier to just film *on* the beach?' And he had laughed and said, 'Real doesn't look as good.' He must have felt sorry for her shivering half to death in a warehouse in mid-November in a thong, because he'd gone and snatched her a dressing gown from wardrobe. She hadn't realised they would charge her for it. They'd gone on a date, she and the key grip, but when he found out what her other job was, he'd never called her back. They never do. Sirens don't tend to reel in the keepers.

Now, she watches herself fill the whole side of the wall in a lime green bikini, playfully flicking water at the camera, lips parted, legs wide, dead eyes. They'd CGI'd her with the three big t's; tan, tushy and tits. No wonder MarKBigBoy4U never recognised her. She looked like a fourteen-year-old boy had wished upon a star for his blow-up doll to be a real girl.

She wondered if there was a programme full of beautiful young men with bottles of knock-off champagne sprayed at their faces, their arses, their crotches?

She didn't have time to check.

20 MINUTES UNTIL CONTRACT COMPLETION.
Be more GlobalHyperMegaCorp™.

She changes the programme to the woodland scene; towering trees, bird calls, endless green. She found it helped, kept them calm. Soothed.

When MarKBigBoy4U surfaces, she is vaping on the edge of the bed. Even the smoke was baby blue, and the air reeked of bubble gum. She'd reapplied her make-up and her lips are the same shade as her dressing gown, Extinction Red: 'Because he's worth it'.

He pulls out the bullet, drops it to the floor and tries to focus. 'Time?'

'More than enough, Sugar Lump,' she lies.

He takes the vape from her, frowning at the lipstick stain. 'I don't pay *Coke-A-Cola* prices to get *Rola Cola*.'

She bites her tongue. Not long now.

She runs her hand up his leg, higher and higher. 'I thought you liked red?' Knowing it had been the preference he'd clicked on the form. Along with 'blonde', 'long legs', and 'must laugh at my jokes'.

'Does it sound like I like it?'

15 MINUTES. GlobalHyperMegaCorp™:
changing the world one consumer at a time.

Big smiles.

She presses the colour tab and the *Be the New You* Dressing Gown changes into a blushing pink. She asks with a single eyebrow arch if it's ok? He grunts his pleasure.

She can see him relax as he draws deep on his man-child vape. He demands a drink, blowing smoke into her face, stinging her eyes. Swinging the glass his way, he seems upset that she'd already thought of it, that she wouldn't have to toddle over to the mini bar and bend over. His days of demanding that were over. The *Forever Ice* smashes against the glass as he downs it.

10 MINUTES. Damage to the commodity will
result in deductions.

She plays his favourite song. '*Price Gun Death Spiral* by Pop Band 10^2.' She had laughed when he'd told her.

'What's so funny?'

And before she could stop herself, she had answered, 'It's ironic, that's all.'

He'd rolled his eyes at her and then explained what irony was. She purred at him how clever he was. How so very God damn *clever*.

The pop-hypnotic tune slides out from hidden speakers.

5

She dances for him, blowing kisses because, despite everything, he was one of the better ones, one of the nicer ones and why not give him the five-star treatment one last time?

4

He tells her it's a right tune, not like the crap that band produces now. *How* they didn't get it. *How* they'd sold out. *Capitalist conformists.*

3

She straddles him, her thighs sticking to the clammy folds of his stomach fat, pressing her lips against his forehead. Smearing extinction red right into the creases.

2

'I couldn't agree more, Sugar Lump.'

1: DON'T FORGET TO INPUT CUSTOMER SATISFACTION.

Time, Gentlemen, please.

She smiles, and for the first time all weekend, it reaches her eyes. He doesn't notice the difference.

She stretches for the secret button behind the headboard. A small door opens. He turns to see what she's doing, but she forces his gaze towards the trees, to the forest, to the evergreen.

Her fingers find it.

He grunts, grabbing at her breasts. His thumb presses into her *GlobalHyperMegaCorp*^{TM} trademarked logo. 18% of everything she earns is sacrificed to that altar. To the organisation that already owns everything.

She lifts the *Bolt Gun 1000*: 'First Time, Every Time'. Careful not to be seen.

'Hashtag happy?' She asks, placing it just behind his ear, close but not touching.

'Smiley face,' he answers.

'Your feedback has been invaluable.' A light pull of the trigger and a hundred pounds of energy is blasted into his brain.

A blissful smile. A trickle of blood spreads over the pillowcase.

Peeling away from him, she wipes the brain tissue from the barrel and places the gun back into the compartment before clicking the door shut.

She rings it in.

Changing the song to Pop Band 10^2's new album, she sits and listens for a while, vaping. He was right; they had sold out, but then, as she wipes a stray spatter of blood from her trademarked logo, she thinks, who hasn't?

She dresses, placing the dressing gown in the wardrobe; it would last another day. Save herself the extra deduction. She had thought about buying her own, but the price was shameless, and so she rents.

She flicks through the endless stream of different TV programmes she can enjoy.

Feel Every Hit at the Ringside.

Know What you're Made of at Everest.

Underwater Dolphin Adventure, and so much more. Every single one had a porn option.

She wonders if *Friends Rebooted* is programmed in, but before she can check, there is a knock on the door. Nervous, she opens it. This would be her first time with the new procedure. She lets in the Processor.

A man in red overalls and a pink afro stuffed into a hair net strides in, 12-H embroidered on his chest. Carrying a hand-held cool box with the words *GlobalHyperMegaCorp^{TM} property*' stamped on the side, his gaze sweeps the room. 'Problems?'

She shakes her head.

She starts collecting the half-eaten takeaway boxes. If the freezer was working, there was enough to feed her for several weeks. It was always a trade-off, maximise the client's weight or leave enough for leftovers. She always chose the latter. Wrapping up the last spring rolls, she asks, 'We met at induction, right?'

'Don't want to be rude, but they've cut the time I have to do this.' He removes a screen from his pocket and reels off questions, inputting her answers.

'Full treatment?'

'Yes.'

'Next of kin?'

'No.'

'Slaughter?'

'Stress-free.'

12-H places the screen back in his pocket. 'They'll deduct you.'

Her hand freezes mid-swipe of the salt and pepper fries. 'Seriously?'

He throws her a sympathetic look. 'New policy. Biofuel, they use the leftover food to power the platinum members' heated swimming pool. Makes it carbon neutral.'

She slumps, back to the *Just Like Mama Used to Make Glucose Pills* then. No more than six a day. Always read the label.

'I suppose new refurbs don't pay for themselves.'

She switches off the TVs and dead screens surround them. She looks small in the reflection, thin, but then the *GlobalHyperMega-Corp*^{TM} logo pops up and she disappears.

12-H opens the box, snapping on a pair of rubber gloves and pulls out a plastic sheet. With a sweaty effort they roll MarKBig-Boy4U onto it. 12-H then gets his scalpel out.

'Jesus, you're doing that *here*?'

He forces a flyaway curl back under his hair net. 'Processing labs don't pay for themselves either. Lost out to the entertainment team, more profitable.' A shrug. 'My lab's a mini-Golf now.' Cutting through the commodity formerly known as MarKBigBoy4U, he removes the organ. Pale and fat, he places it in the cool box, and waits for the all-important number to pop up. 'Nice! Heaviest yield I've had all week.' A ticket is printed off and handed over. An0nymuse6 beams at the amount.

12-H flicks off the gloves, closes the lid, and locks it with his finger ID. Done.

'That's it?' She pockets the ticket. 'I always thought it would be more technical than that.'

'It's pretty simple. The rest of him just goes down the new chute system with the leftovers.'

A bitter smile. 'To heat the outdoor swimming pool?'

'To heat the outdoor swimming pool.'

It had been easy to get MarKBigBoy4U to sign himself away for the cheap, cheap price of eight Face-2-Face Full-Access Weekends. The Girlfriend Experience. 50% discount if he signed right there and then. Which he did. He saw the below-market rate for a call girl, felt the blood rush and ticked away at that, 'I agree to the Terms and Conditions' box.

Now the eight weekends were up, and he belonged to *GlobalHyperMegaCorp™*, although at least his contract had ended. An0nymuse6 was still paying off that pesky bout of trying to save her Mum from cancer. She hadn't. She thinks about closing MarKBigBoy4U's eyes, but 12-H hurries her out of the room. 'Thirty seconds before the strip and dump. They can't start it till we're out, and if you're not...'

'I know, I know, deductions.'

They move down the freshly painted hallway, 12-H setting the pace and An0nymuse6 jogging alongside to keep up, she holds out her hand. 'I'm...'

But a voice on the Processor's digital auditor interrupts,

> 43 SECONDS BEHIND SCHEDULE. We value our
> processing associates, have a
> GlobalHyperMegaCorp™ day.

He speeds off with the liver, muttering how he had another sixteen to process today.

She stands in the hallway alone, her bag empty and limp by her side. She smells of new sweat and greasy food and suddenly wants to cry.

She thinks about the tiny flat filled with books, about the girl who grows daffodils and plaited her hair. Her smile. A smile that seemed so... natural, so free. An0nymuse6 imagines leaving the hotel and crossing the street to her building, making her way up the stairs, roaming the high-rise corridors, speeding past grey door after grey door, but right at the end of the hallway, it's there, painted in yellow or maybe blue. She can hear singing from the other side, can smell pasta cooking, like her Mum used to make. She pictures lifting her hand to knock, but then what would she even say? 'Hi, I'm a siren sex worker, love your vibe babe.'

> NOTIFICATION. NEW MESSAGE. Remember you are the face of GlobalHyperMegaCorp™, so smile.

An0nymuse6 pulls up the message; it's her latest catch, Smilies_-Suck89, seeing if she was free for a chat? Her finger hovers over the reply button, suddenly unsure. Hashtag happy?

Her stomach rumbles.

She messages Smilies_Suck89: 'Always for you, Sugar Lump.'

Quick as you like he sends back. 'Three kissy faces and an eggplant...' Oh, wait, and a dick pic. A dead cert. She sighs; another kilo and a half of free-range, cruelty-free foie gras from your friendly *GlobalHyperMegaCorp™*; 'The best money can buy'.

Terms and conditions apply.

THE EIGHTH SACRAMENT

P J WHITELEY

'Excuse me. Miss! Young lady! I think you've dropped something.'

She turns around. Looks down. She has been hurrying, reluctant to stop, head down. Her chain of beads is on the ground. The formation betrays their heresy: the family of three beads on an appendage, plus one either side, the five decades in a coil of spirals and circles, a Celtic cross in cheap metal, a corner missing.

He picks it up, examines it like evidence, offers a slight smile and hands it to her.

'I'm sorry, I, er thank you.' She snatches them from the young man's outstretched hand, a little too abruptly, apologizes again. Her eyes, green and glinting with fire and ice; they dart outwards and up towards him. Dark curly hair falls from her forehead. His eyes are dark blue, calmer. 'I'm sorry,' she says. 'I'm not, er, What I mean to say is –' She glances sideways in place of completing her sentence. She glances then to the other side, briefly watches a group of grumbling, shouting men stumble out of the tavern. Then she looks at the young man.

'It's fine,' he says. 'I mean no ill-will. I'm not, what I mean to say is, I'm not like... '

'Seems neither of us is sure what we mean to say.'

'You need to get home safe. I wouldn't go past that tavern tonight.' He nods towards the Star, a white-painted building, part of a long terrace, on the opposite side of the road. More men are spilling out of the building.

'My family knows not to go in there, but I've walked past it often enough.'

'Not tonight, it's not safe, especially for, well you know. There's trouble brewing.'

'So I've heard. That's why I'm rushing. Mrs Latchford let me go early.'

'You work in the store?'

'Yes. Listen, I must be on my way. Thank you for returning the beads.'

'But, I don't mean to intrude, but the route you're heading on isn't safe. Especially for, well I thought it only fair to warn you.'

'And why should you care?'

His eyes widen with curiosity. They look at each other. 'Why does anyone care about anything?'

She does not reply, takes half a step one way, an even smaller step another.

'We'll go down this side street?'

'*We?*' she is alarmed.

'I'm sorry. I really mean no ill-will. You ought to stay safe.'

'What? Can I trust you? Are you trying to take advantage?'

'No, no, no! I swear I'm not. I'm a Christian, brought up to treat ladies with respect.'

'Well it's nice to be called a lady, I must say, but I really should make my own way home.'

A rumbling noise grows louder as the mob emerge onto the road, heading towards them, gaining pace, beginning to charge. There are over 100, swollen in numbers as the taverns are emptied. Most of the crowd are holding clubs, several have torches held high aloft, flames leaping high with desire and spite. She can hear the words 'Fenian', 'death' and 'go home'.

'Right you are, well. I mean...' she has run out of words, and options.

'It's me or the mob.'

The side street is narrow, they walk its length. Horse manure lies thick and plentiful in the centre, the trail of an earlier escape route, the thick odour fills the thin space. At the end they double back on a parallel street to resume their direction but they reach a cross street, Broadway. There is another crowd here, even larger and more furious. A horse neighs and whinnies in fear. Windows are closed, curtains drawn.

They are about to enter the next side street when a gang of six men approach them. They are a mix of young and middle aged, glassy-eyed. The eldest is holding a torch, but it is becoming too heavy for him and the flames are close to his hair and ear.

A younger man addresses them: 'Get your young lady home and come join us.'

He does not reply, just smiles and nods. As he does so, she moves closer to him, almost touching.

The man continues: 'Rid the town of Fenians and priestcraft. Are you not with us, are you one of them?'

'Just making our way home.'

'You're not from here. You Scottish?'

'Yorkshire.'

'Right enough. Not Ireland. Is she from Yorkshire too?'

'Yes.'

'Pretty.' The stranger moves close to her.

'We're just trying to get home.'

'Very pretty.' Looks her up and down.

'Don't come any closer.'

'Woah! There's a Yorkie here thinks he can take us all on.'

'Step away, Jack,' says one of the older men. 'They're not our problem.'

'Which side are you on though?' the younger man shouts as the group walk away to rejoin the throng. 'Which side are you on?'

The two of them are left together. They breathe deeply.

'Well done for not saying anything,' he says.

'Well done for not hitting him.'

'I told a lie.'

'That I was from Yorkshire? It was a good lie, right enough.'

'It was, wasn't it?'

'Don't go making a habit of it.'

They enter the narrow side lane, parallel to Broadway, past cottages, blessedly quiet, they cross a field. She follows him, then they walk side by side. They agree a route.

'We have a cottage on the landowner's field,' she says. 'So we can go all the way around the town, without going back in.'

In the countryside now, they turn to cross the road that is the continuation of Broadway, cast anxious glances both ways, and scurry across and into the field on the other side, opening and closing a large gate. Thick hawthorn hedges hide them from view. The grass is yellowing, the ground firm and unyielding. A few sheep trot away as they enter.

'You don't sound very, I mean ... your accent sounds almost local,' he says.

'I don't sound very Irish, you mean.'

'No.'

'I picked up the local one, as much as I could.'

'To blend in.'

'To blend in.'

'Until you drop your rosary beads.'

'Yes, that's a giveaway.'

'Listen, I've worked on the railways. I work with folk from all backgrounds. I had Irish gangs on the viaduct, they're good workers. Good lads.'

'You an engineer?'

'Yes, qualified now.'

She says nothing. He says: 'The railway is finished now.'

'You must feel very proud. Have you travelled on it?'

'Yes,' he replies.

'What's it like?'

'Smoky and you rattle around, but mighty fast. Just two hours to Birmingham.'

'Why would you want to go to Birmingham?'

He is amused. 'Well for work, or to see a show. Or get a train to London.'

'London!' She pauses and thinks. 'In the future,' she says, 'Will you be able to get the train directly to London from Shropshire?'

'Oh, I doubt that.'

'Oh. That's disappointing. I think I shan't bother with the railway.'

'You can go to Holyhead and Liverpool now,' he suggests. 'Visit Ireland.'

She just looks at him, like he had suggested the moon.

'You don't want to return, ever, see relatives?' he asks.

'They're all dead.'

'Visit your village, your town?'

'It doesn't exist any more.'

They say nothing for a while. The noise of the crowd rises for a while then dims, then rises again as a throaty roar. It is the voice of a single being now. Their route is a three-quarter circle, never too far from the town centre. There is a noise of kindling splitting and cracking. The torches, as well as the crowd, are beginning to merge. At times a few flames flicker and leap above the line of the hedgerows.

'My friend Milburga Flanagan has a cousin by marriage called Ryan Eyre,' she says. 'He's the only one who's gone back to Ireland for a visit.'

'He sounds enterprising and adventurous.'

'Apparently he's cheap and unreliable. She doesn't trust him. Gift of the Blarney, mind.'

'So your family is all here. Do you have any brothers and sisters?'

She says nothing some more, but opens her mouth as if to begin, then closes it, then opens it again. He is calm in his silence, just looks ahead. She fidgets.

Eventually, she asks: 'Why do they hate us?'

'I, I don't know. Hatred has no reason. There are attitudes I hear, but they don't seem a reason for hatred, to me.'

'Where did you hear the rumours about trouble tonight? Were you in the tavern earlier?'

'No. I don't drink. My family doesn't. My Dad calls it the demon.'

'Well, he's got a point. He'd like my ma and da.'

They walk quietly some more; she is fidgeting, he is calm. 'Why are you helping me?' she asks.

'I don't like the drunks and the ruffians. They bring shame on our folk. You should get home safe. It's how I was raised.'

'What do they say about us?'

'You don't want to know.'

'No. I do.'

'You really don't.'

'Well, maybe not all of it,' she hesitates, but continues. 'I don't like not knowing.'

'They say the Irish are drunken, filthy and lazy.'

'So, you get the Irish over to build your tunnels and embankments and railway lines and then you call us lazy? Make your mind up.'

'You make a fair point!' He chuckles. 'It's not what I say. I'm just repeating what I hear. Like I say, I had Irish folk on my teams building the viaduct. Good lads. Hardest workers we had.'

'What else?'

'That you'd want to replace Parliament with the Pope.'

'That's all I hear from English folk. Does the Pope make you do this? Does the Pope say that? What does the Pope think of this? They think about what the Pope says and does more than we do.'

She becomes animated, stumbles for a moment on a high tuft of grass. He begins to reach out a hand to help steady her, and with-draws it as she regains her balance. They both pause for a moment. He wipes his brow with the back of his hand, she does the same. They continue. The ground is hard, unyielding. Bare of grass in small patches. The sheep bleat and moan.

'They say you have icons, worship false gods,' he continues. 'Again, this is what they say, not what I say.'

'I like to have our Lady looking down, and clutch my beads.'

'You don't feel you're worshipping, well, objects, icons?'

'It's not worship, it's comfort.' She pulls out her rosary, clutches the beads, prays under her breath.

'You have lots of candles, so they say.'

'Well look around you tonight! The Protestant candles are a lot bigger!'

'True enough. And you honour the saints, is that correct? They all have their own day? Sorry, am I asking too many questions?'

'No, it sounds like you're just curious. Why don't Protestants like saints? Even the best ones? Saint Anthony and Saint Francis?'

'I don't know about them.'

'Isn't it a good thing now that a man can be strong and brave and kind-hearted too?' They stop and she looks at him, holds his gaze; knows she shouldn't, blushes, looks down.

'I agree,' he replies. 'It is a fine combination in a man. Rare enough.' Again, that calm smile, so comforting it unsettles her. His face is sweaty, two-day old beard. His pale shirt is grimy at the edges, clean in the middle, sleeves rolled up, revealing curved biceps. A cloth belt holds his trousers up. They are work clothes.

'What else do they say?' she asks.

'Are you sure you want to know?'

'Yes. It is education.'

'It's not all the English, you know, who say these things.'

'I know. Mrs Latchford is kind. Many people have been.'

'Some say the Irish are suppressing wages, under-cutting the locals.'

'They could give us all a wage rise, then. That'd solve that problem.'

'In England we have a saying: Hard work never killed anyone.'

'Do you now?'

'It's not true of course. Hard work killed most folk I know.'

'You work hard, don't you?'

'I learned a skill. That makes a difference.'

'Hard work and no food,' she says. 'That's the worst.'

'They say the hunger was the fault of the Irish themselves. Single crop, poor farming, then refused to work for their relief.'

'There was no relief. There was plenty of hard labour mind.'

'And that the Irish are a threat to the Protestant way, to law and order. They should be transported.'

'So they get the Irish in to build the transport, so that we can all be transported out again. Tell me now, how did the British build an empire?'

They resume walking, silent for a while, then she says: 'So, in your church do you have sin, and hell, and sacraments?'

'Not sacraments.'

'We have seven, I've had four. Baptism, first confession, first communion, confirmation.'

'What are the other three?'

'Marriage, ordination and last rites.'

'Marriage next on the list, then.'

Silence.

He tries again. 'Ordination. Is that an option for you?'

She pulls a face. 'I'm not sure the world is need of more nuns, to be honest.'

He laughs. She says nothing.

He tries again. 'Why seven?'

'I don't know. I didn't make the rules.'

'Who did? The Pope?'

'There you go again!' she says, raising her voice slightly, but more amused than annoyed. 'The Pope this, the Pope that. Protestants! You're obsessed with the Pope!'

He laughs, guttural, involuntary. She is startled, glances sideways and up at him, uncertain, looking for signs of mockery. His returned gaze is warm. She opts to say nothing, gives a small grin, assured, she hopes. *Yes, I was hoping for a laugh. Wry humour is what I do.* Keeps her smile as she fixes her gaze ahead, hitches up her long pale shabby dress out of the dried grass.

They reach a stile at the end of the field. He climbs over first. She lifts up her skirt to clamber over. She places both feet on the wooden step on the opposite side and looks down. He begins to lift his hand to offer it, changes his mind and lowers it. She gives a little jump into the field, then strides off along a diagonal through the sheep field. They are closer to the town again, and a louder cheer erupts with violence near to them. The spitting of the flames is more rapid and furious.

The fire rises as the sun sets. All moisture is sucked from the air. A parched hatred. The embers rise and fly, dance and spiral and fall. Sent skywards with hatred, they fall with a strange grace. They fall on dried-out mud and yellowed grass; on startled sheep and on indifferent sheep, on hedges, stones, walls, and roofs. They fall and they lie where they fall; without agency, they die meekly.

They enter the next field, which is a field of wheat, greenish shoots struggling for height with the drought, and they skirt around the edge, stumbling through the narrow space on hardened soil between crop and hedgerow. This part of the route brings them closer again to Broadway. They can hear individual shouts, foul curses and threats, see individual torches bobbing with movement, then thrown high onto a central inferno. The fire has launched itself higher, great sheets of flame, not mere tongues. It is worshipped by the crowd, like a show. The roof has gone.

The horror draws their attention again. Their faces are lit up by the fire.

'Is that the... ?' she asks, unable to complete the sentence.

'The house on Broadway,' he says.

'Where Father Molloy says mass on a Sunday.'

'Yes.'

'So that's the target,' she says in a level voice, absorbing the implication.

'There's no one inside?' he asks.

'I don't know.'

They stand and watch, side by side. They do not want to watch, they are compelled.

'Disgraceful. A place of worship, too. They bring shame on us. In our family we were brought up better. I'm sorry. I'm so, so sorry.'

'Is this how things will be from now on?' she asks. 'Will this be every week? Will we have nowhere to say mass? Will they come after our homes next?'

'I don't know. The magistrates and Lord Stafford must put a stop to this.'

Their voices are formal, there is no eye contact. She glances sideways up at him, opens her mouth to begin a statement, but stays silent. They begin to walk again; as they reach the further end of the field they have put some distance between them and the pyre. The heat and the voices subside in volume. They walk in silence for a short while, but then there is a huge cracking noise, as a beam from the building is broken by the flames, collapses. There is a cheer, a deep guttural cheer, from the mob. They turn again to witness the horror.

'Strange how the agents of law and order bring chaos wherever they go,' he says.

'Isn't it just?'

Her hand brushes against his, and his against hers. It is an accident. She pulls hers away, looks down.

'I just hope my ma and da are home safe.'

'Yes, we should carry on. I'll see you there.'

'Yes, please.'

They enter another field of wheat, walking around the edge again, just inside the hedgerow. 'We're probably trespassing,' he says.

'I've walked this way often enough.'

'I think Lord Stafford owns this land.'

'What does it mean, now, to own land?' she asks.

'Well, the right to farm it.'

'If you own the land, do you own the hedges and the trees?'

'Yes, I think so.'

'What about the birds in the trees, or flying above?'

'No, not those.'

'So you own the land itself, but not the air above it? So while the soles of my shoes are trespassing, the rest of me is not.'

He smiles. 'You would make a fine lawyer.'

'The law is only for rich people. They own the land, they own the magistrates.'

'Without ownership and the law, there would be a free-for-all for rogues and thieves.'

'I daresay you're right.'

'Anyway, Lord Stafford is Catholic, so they say.'

'They won't be burning down his chapel, I don't suppose.'

'No. I guess rich folk can pray how they like.'

'Lord Stafford looks out for us,' she observes.

'He is a fine gentleman, so I hear.'

'Yes. I won't have a word said against him.'

'Nor will I.'

'Well that's settled then.'

'Yes.'

'One more field to go.' They have reached another stile.

'Strange, you showing me around,' he says. 'Like you're the local.'

'I've lived here five years. Our future is here now, if the locals will let us stay. My ma and da can't speak much English, but they want me to. They buy books for me, they've done so ever after we came to England, like an obsession. They don't know what they are buying. So I get a romantic book, then a textbook on botany, then an adventure story, then a history. They started a school, back in Ireland, in our village. Before – well, before.'

This silence is the longest.

'Do you imagine Lord Stafford has rosary beads?' he asks, after a while.

'Probably!'

'I wonder what they're made of. Pearls, or gold. He would have to keep them well hidden in the House of Lords.'

'Keeps them out of sight as he says extra Hail Marys before his speech. That is, if he ever gets nervous. Do you think rich people get nervous?'

'I think everyone does,' he replies.

'Even the mob?'

'Especially the mob.' He pauses, then adds: 'Listen, this will pass. I'm sure this will pass. Everything is temporary.'

'Some things endure.' She is acquainted with the steady relentlessness of time, its unbiased measure and slow healing.

'There are always good people, too.'

They have reached the terraced row of tiny rural cottages, on the edge of the farm. Hers is at the end. She turns around. She says: 'I did have brothers and a sister, back in Ireland.' Her eyes are no longer piercing, they are drowning in their own sea, overflowing down her cheeks.

'I'm sorry,' he says, simply.

'Don't make me say their names.'

His chest and shoulders sag and he bows his head. After a pause he looks up again. 'Please, I'm sorry. My condolences. I'm glad you're home safe. I'll go unless you want me to wait for you to check your folks are well and safe.'

'You've done all you can, thank you. There's a candle on. I'm sure they're fine.'

'A good safe Catholic candle. It's getting dark, finally. I'll go, then.'

'Thank you.'

'I'm Angus, by the way. Angus Rawnsley.'

'Maria Kenny. Thank you for your help.'

'It's no bother.'

'No, it really was. You went out of your way. You're a credit to your parents. Thank you.'

'It's fine. I'm no saint.'

'Not yet, anyway,' she replies, and she smiles, for the first time that day, or that year, or indeed, in many years.

He smiles and nods, turns to go.

Author's note: This story is dedicated to the memory of Maria Kenny and Angus Rawnsley, my great-grandparents. Angus converted from Anglicanism to Catholicism and married Maria. This story is fiction – the real Angus and Maria were a generation younger than the versions portrayed in this story. Maria's parents in real life, Mary née Naughton and Thomas Kenny, born respectively in Mayo and Roscommon, were living in Shifnal, Shropshire at the time of the anti-Irish riot on 30 June 1855, in which the house on Broadway used for Catholic masses was burned down.

SPLINTERS

MARK BOWSHER

The sharp coldness of ice, a freezing wire, pulled tight, cutting my heart in two.
    I feel it.
A warning.
My good hand stops, palm flat, ready to rap on the door, shrivelled leaves whipped about by the storm brushing my torn skin.

The sudden downpour has cut me off from the village. Too deep in the woods, too lost, turning and turning and twisting and twisting – I may be feet away from the path home, but all sense of direction has deserted me as the tempest bites. I must find shelter, or my tale ends here.

This place, a dwelling caught in the maze of the woods, a thick canopy above making day and night indistinguishable, looks abandoned. Nothing about it is inviting, but the alternative is to drown, become frozen, be battered to death in this squall. I have no choice.

I rap and call out, hoarse cries from my raw throat. My other hand sits at the end of a limp arm, crushed and bloody, the splinters digging in, pulsating with pain as my good hand smacks against the thick wooden door.

It opens.

I step within but no warmth follows. No crackle of fire from the hearth, no bleat from the sheep munching hay in the corner, as I would find in my own dwelling. Just stark silence. Somehow it is darker inside, the windows coated in vines. Chairs, tables, workbenches, but no life. No dust, no rot. The dry emptiness of death.

I close the door and sense my newfound shelter recoiling, as if I am a bitterness on the tongue. Its silence is a judgement. The throbbing pain in my smashed hand and my stuttering breaths make me feel too alive in this haunted stillness. I toy apprehensively with the splinters embedded in my swollen flesh. I hope William has taken the flock into the house for the night, though I doubt the pack hunts in this storm. I must sleep, be dead for the night and pray for healing come the morning.

Sit.

Comes the voice and I obey, the weighty chair immovable as I collapse into it.

Rest.

It creeps out of nowhere, sharp and high, blending in with the shiver of branches, the crinkle of leaves, the creak of the trees, the groan of the wind-whipped house.

Splint.

The word buries itself in my mind. I search for meaning. I find it. I spy the wooden splint on the bare table and strap it to my wounded arm, tearing off shreds of my mangled tunic to fasten it in place. I wince, sucking in breath through my teeth, the bruises echoing with pain at even the slightest touch. I flinch as my fingers brush the splinters, burying them deeper.

I taste the air of this place. Dank, sour, lifeless. I retract the thought that this place is dead. To perish you must first live. The worktops are bare, the chairs far from the table, the windows high, the latches out of reach. Whoever built this place did not entertain the notion that someone would live here.

Ressst...

'Can I stay the night?'

It is already morning.

I look up once more and spy the vine-coated windows, which do not unveil the secret of day beyond the canopy.

Rest until you are ready.

I drift away into a dream, a numbed recreation of the misfortune that led me here flitting through my mind.

Upon waking, barely able to move, I become preoccupied with locating and removing splinters. I wince and suck air through my teeth.

Do not remove them.

The voice. It was not my mind. Not the delirium of an injured fool upon the brink of collapse.

'Don't remove them?'

Only an imbecile repeats what he heard so clearly not a moment before.

You will do more harm by taking them out.

I cease.

'Do you know the way back to the village?'

It considers. I look about. One room. No bed. No hearth. Nowhere to hide, no solitary figure crouched in the shadows amongst the rafters above.

You must chop wood.

'I must return home!' I insist. I wonder if William has let the sheep and chickens back outside for the day yet.

You cannot leave until you are well. You cannot stay if you do not work.

'If I'm not well enough to walk home then I'm not well enough to chop wood.'

You cannot leave until you are well.

It leaves the rest unsaid. The howl of the wind and the creak of the house and trees fill the silence between me and the other.

After some minutes, I suck in all my pain and weariness and head outside.

The wind whips around me. I feel the elements tugging at the splinters to be free, but they remain, burrowed into my skin. I see an axe, lying on its side on the ground, its blade not buried in the wood to protect the woodchopper from cutting himself in the dark. I wonder who placed it there. I look around to see if the voice has a face. None presents itself.

I wonder if William has emptied the shit bucket into the river or knocked it over again. If only this was the day's predicament.

There are no flickers of light slinking down through the crisscross of the canopy. Perhaps it is cloudy, maybe it is night. It is hard to say. My eyes are accustomed to the dark now.

I sigh deeply once more, lift the axe and get to work.

Splinters fly high, finding new homes in my skin. With each strike, I feel the pain of the gashes I inflict on the wood reverberate through my crumpled limb. I catch my breath as the excruciating sensation spreads, like fresh bruises under the skin of my broken hand. Then I chop and chop and work through the pain. I scream, louder and louder as my strikes land harder and harder.

My good hand is tired. I transfer the axe into my swollen grip and hack away, as I throb with pain.

A guttural cry, my throat shredded, my eyes shut tight. I miss the tree, the axe swings round and back towards my other shoulder. I slice through skin, through flesh and muscle, break bone and crumple onto the ground to my left in defeat, my dismembered arm taking a different path. The agony is white hot and instant. We bleed in unison, the red of my life flowing faster from my fresh stump than from the discarded appendage thanks to my screaming heart.

I am lost and dizzy yet all too aware of my predicament. Leaf and moss and twigs I claw at, gathering them together, and I hold it all against the wound, blood congealing with the detritus of the forest floor.

I do not recall how I managed to crawl back into the house, yet somehow I returned here.

It is no warmer, barely quieter, yet still I pretend I am better within than without. The pain has numbed, my head is swirling. I keep staring at the bloody stump, coated in leaf, moss and twig, sucking in the unreality of it.

Hush.

The voice once more, the speaker unseen.

Sleep. You will be better when you wake.

'Please! Find someone from the village!' I wonder if William has come looking for me.

What is your village like?

'It's at the end of the path!'

Is it peaceful? Are the people kind?

'Please!'

Are they kind? Do you have a sweetheart?

I am halted in my desperate thoughts. I see her face.

'Yes.'

Is she beautiful?

'Yes.'

Tell me of her.

'She has raven hair, skin paler than the milk she churns. When she smiles, her plump cheeks stick out, and she is beautiful.'

Have you shared a bed with her?

'We are not married!'

I understand. Have you shared a bed with her?

'...I have.'

Dream on that. Let it warm you. You will be well come the morning.

I regard the messy stump again. My head is swimming, drowning in the mental fuzz.

The pain comes and goes in flushes. I think of her, of the village and of the fields and the foothills of the mountains and of all the places I have ever been. I would be there again. I drift away, pondering whether beyond the canopy is a blazing sun or a haunting moon.

Waking comes suddenly. The world wraps itself around me.

I am here still, in the unlived-in house. There is a smell; warm, comforting and familiar. Pottage. A wooden bowl on the table, the steam rising and meandering, inviting me to dine. I lean forward greedily and my hand creaks.

I look. There it is, perfectly carved, smoother than skin, deep oak brown, immobile fingers at its farthest reach.

Do you like it?

'You made this?'

The voice does not answer. It waits.

Eat.

I look from my wooden limb to my puffy broken hand. The splint is tied tight, but I am becoming accustomed to it now. I turn back to my new appendage. I try to remember how I first learned to move my fingers, but the knowledge does not return to me. And just as I think I cannot retrain myself, my fresh fingers creak, fan out and I wiggle them playfully.

I begin to eat, caring not that the hot pottage is burning my throat. My wooden arm feels heavy and difficult to manoeuvre, though with each mouthful it becomes easier.

'Will you help me find my way home?'

Of course. Is it busy there? Always buzzing with activity? Friendly faces around every corner?

'Yes.'

Wonderful... You must miss it.

'I do.'

Then we must make you strong again. You see the tree outside? There is a fruit on the top branch.

'I cannot climb up there!'

No, of course. You must fashion a ladder to help you reach the top.

'A ladder? I can barely lift my bad hand! And the new one...the new arm...I am not yet used to it.'

You will heal. You will adjust. Give it time.

'But...'

Your footsteps shall be heard on the street leading through your village soon.

I nod. I am in pain and cannot argue. I follow its commands.

I find tools outside. I chop and chop, taking care not to injure myself again. If only William was here to help, I would not be shouting and shaking my head at him this time.

My bad hand is indeed better, though the splinters have increased in number. And they are thicker. They protrude from my skin, almost as thick as twigs now. I tie the splint tighter and no longer wince, becoming attuned to the pain.

I chop and chop and chop. My new hand is supple and strong. It is part of me now. I chop and chop and chop and chop. Though I am careful. I will not lose my other arm. I chop and cut and sand.

Soon the steps take shape and I affix them to two long shafts. I am slowing. Some fresh pain is spreading. I sand and sand and sand and a snow of yellow sawdust engulfs my feet. The pain is spreading.

All of a sudden, a panic takes me over. I must locate the source of the pain. I move my foot out of the heap of sawdust and the heap moves with me. I tear open the hem of my trousers. My leg! All the way up to the knee it is coated in sawdust. I brush it off. Brush-brush-brush-and-brush! It will not shift. A dizziness claims me. The day is done.

———

I awake.

I grope with my healing hand. The tearing pain of the splinters, now thick as fingers, digging into my skin. The wood of the splint sits comfortably against my flesh now.

With great trepidation, my shaking hand searches for my leg. I run my hand along the skin and feel the immovable layer of sawdust coating the limb. The splinters in my fingers catch as I run them over the surface, tugging at the wounds they have created.

Are there meadows there? Fields to run through and dance in?
'Yes.'

Streams to bathe in, and wood for fires, and an inn full of jollity, and encounters with lovers to be had?
'Yes.'

And houses with beds, and tables to sit at and enjoy a simple yet filling meal?
'Yes.'

And conversations to be had! Will you talk about death and life and adventures and rivers and mountains and love and stars and wonders?
'Yes. All of that.'

You must miss it.
'Yes.'

The fruit...
'At the top of the tree...?'

The very top...
I blink. A figure lingers in my periphery.

I turn yet no one is there. Not a wisp of a shadow. Nowhere to hide

I must leave this place.

I stand. My new limb creaks as I hobble across the floorboards, wood on wood.

I push open the door with my healing hand. The splinters do not catch, they are part of me now and they no longer hurt. They are natural. They are skin.

I see the tree, greet it with a nod as if it is my kin. I climb the ladder and into the tree. I creak with the branches in the wind. I am heavy, but slowly I haul my own weight. In the dim light my arms are indistinguishable from the branches. My fingers are twigs and my abdomen the bough.

I see the fruit, up high, shining and red. I reach out. I know before it happens that I will fall, as if all is now slower, all is inevitable. I am part of the forest and time's heart beats with the rise and fall of the sun here. Bud to sprout to slim bough to towering tree, lording over the forest.

I plummet, and as I land, twig and moss and leaf are hurled up into the air. They cover me and press into my flesh as I lie there, snapped and cracked and bleeding, my sap pouring out as pain shoots through my broken form...

...Your skin is weak and transitory...
   ...Bark is tough...
   ...It will protect you in all weathers...
   ...You breathe with the forest now...

I am here and I am nowhere.

I go to open my eyes but there are no eyes to open. I go to move but there is no me to move. And yet I see. I take in this place from above. The room all around me. It is here and I am here and we are all one. My rafters creak with the wind, my eaves contract in the squall, and I ponder on the somewhere where I might be.

'Rest...' says the voice.

Where am I?

'You are home.'

I search for the splinters but there are none.

Where are you?

'I must go now,' the voice was moving with the footsteps treading my floorboards. They are nearing my door now. Their shape is familiar, their form light as flesh. 'I will run in meadows again... I will taste the warmness of milk... I will savour the lover's embrace once more...'

What of me...?

The splinters do not hurt. The splinters do not ache. The splinters are part of me.

The figure moves to my door and then beyond.

'You are home... You are home...'

THE H3 CLASS

NICOLE SWENGLEY

'Paint your emotions, Harriet, it's really not that hard once you get going.' Stephen Warren's instruction was issued in a tone of weary patience accompanied by the softest of sighs.

Harriet's tired eyes dropped to a rectangle of hardboard, surrounded by brushes, squeezed tubes of paint and a small mixing palette. She could feel a lump of disappointment rising in her throat and blinked rapidly to forestall tears.

Heavens! She'd tried so hard to get it right this time. It had taken hours to trawl through old holiday photographs and select a favourite scene – a felucca on the Nile – that would match this week's theme of sky-over-water. She'd spent ages sketching the image repeatedly in pencil before attempting to reproduce it using the brushes and oil-paints.

Capturing the graceful curve of the sail had been easy – her mastery of linear composition came as a surprise – although her attempts to conjure sunlit ripples on the river were clearly less successful. Still, she'd managed to evoke the arid timelessness of the distant landscape; the ancient peace of the place. Wasn't that emotion enough? Clearly not, judging by Stephen Warren's remark.

Her mind flipped back to the initial session when he'd addressed the class and outlined his methods in such a calm, reassuring manner that her anxieties had dribbled away.

'We use the expressive capacity of creating art as a form of psychotherapy,' he'd told his students. 'Try not to feel nervous. You don't need any prior artistic knowledge or experience. Just consider the class a safe space and an opportunity to reflect on life and connect with your emotions. Together we'll reach a place of greater acceptance and appreciation of life.'

Stephen had now reached Sam's table, his hand on the skinny lad's shoulder while he discussed the teenager's painting. 'A vast improvement on last week,' he was saying. 'That blazing sky is terrific and the sea looks wildly angry. Maybe add a touch more titanium white along the surf to lash it up a notch but I can really feel its fury. Good effort, Sam. You found it a cleansing experience, I hope - bringing all that suppressed anger out into the open?'

Sam shrugged and ducked his head, embarrassed by Stephen's praise. 'Yeah, it was wicked,' he replied, shuffling his feet and addressing the remark to his paint-splattered trainers.

Stephen sauntered over to another student then turned and beckoned Harriet to join him. 'Come and look at Lisa's storm. This is exactly what I mean by painting your emotions.'

Lisa's pale face brightened as she moved aside to let Harriet study her work and the carved lines of nervous strain around her eyes momentarily disappeared. Pushing limp, greying hair away from hollow cheeks, she cocked her head on one side in anticipation of her classmate's response.

'Oh!' gulped Harriet, her hand involuntarily rising to her throat. 'It's... ' Shocked by the artwork's choking, bilious colours, caked layers of paint and savagery of execution, she sought in vain for something positive to say.

Unlike her gentle Nile evocation, the watery scene was ominous with menace. Billowing black clouds tore across a sickeningly green sky, below which a lake curdled in poisonous yellow. Indigo trees to one side bent in tortured shapes, their branches twisting like broken limbs. A nightmare, Harriet thought with a shiver. If this chaotic scene reflected Lisa's inner emotions, she would prefer to keep her distance no matter how placidly careworn the older woman seemed on the surface.

'This is what you need to do, Harriet.' The quiet imperative in Stephen's voice was as persistent as a dripping tap. 'Let your subconscious spill out on the canvas. Re-connect with those deeply vulnerable parts of your psyche that need healing. You'll find it remarkably therapeutic.'

'I – I'll try,' she said doubtfully, turning back to her table and eyeing her own painting. Maybe she shouldn't have chosen that wonderful holiday with Ben for inspiration. It had been such a memorable trip yet within a year everything in her life turned sour. Yes, it had been a mistake to paint the past. And why was she keeping that Nile image anyway? She should have deleted all those holiday photos on her computer ages ago. In the same way that Ben had deleted her.

Stephen's voice jarred her back to the present. 'For next week's class we'll be working with charcoal. I want you to try scribble drawing.'

'What's that?' After her moment of stardom with the dramatic storm-scape Lisa was now looking fretful. 'I don't understand what you mean.'

'No need to worry, Lisa. You'll get the hang of it very quickly. You start by moving a stick of charcoal around the paper and keep working away at it until you start to see an image that makes some sense. Then I want you to write down its significance to you.'

'A picture comes out of the scrawl – is that how it works?' Lisa sounded dubious.

'Yes, you'll find it happens automatically. A bit like having the kind of dream that stays with you when you wake up in the morning.'

'After a spliff or two with mates,' muttered Sam with a cheeky grin.

Harriet heard a snigger at the adjacent table. It came from Poppy, the bone-thin twenty-something with whom she'd had a coffee after last week's class. She flashed the younger woman a quick smile and received an exaggerated pout in return.

'Mine will be a complete mess,' said Poppy, a faint whine in her voice.

'No more so than anyone else's drawing,' said Stephen reassuringly.

'So how does the image emerge from the mess?' persisted Poppy.

Stephen gave a dry chuckle. 'You may be surprised to find your subconscious mind works its own magic, Poppy. Out of chaos comes clarity.'

Poppy frowned. 'I don't get it.'

'Well, let's take the example of three overlapping circles. A small one sitting on top of a larger one with a tiny one joined at one side. It could look like pebbles on a beach to Sam and bring back memories of a happy, childhood holiday but you might see a Madonna and Child.'

Harriet felt her hands begin to tremble. Madonna and Child. No, she couldn't go there. She snapped her eyes shut and took a deep breath. Then she took another and counted to six while exhaling slowly before opening her eyes again cautiously. The grief counsellor was right, she thought, realising the moment of panic had passed.

Flicking her eyes towards Stephen, she saw he was packing up, holding out boxes for brushes and tubes of paint as he passed each student. 'Lay your paintings on the table over there and I'll stack them in the store-cupboard when they're dry,' he instructed. 'We can look at them again next week and spend a bit more time on analysis.'

Harriet moved over to Poppy's table. 'May I see?'

Poppy nodded, dabbing some turpentine on a cloth to clean a brush. 'It's abstract,' she said unnecessarily as Harriet studied the painting.

Strands of eye-wateringly bright orange and yellow criss-crossed the hardboard. A rash of livid pink spots had broken out on one corner. Jagged green lines interrupted a bubble of vivid blue whorls at the top while a row of unpleasant, brown, turd-like shapes decorated the lower edge of the rectangle. Was it meant to conjure sky-over-beach? It resembled no abstract Harriet had ever seen at an art exhibition. Howard Hodgkin or Mark Rothko it was not.

Harriet bit her lip. She had no in-depth knowledge of Poppy's personal story but she'd gleaned her teenage years had been dominated by drugs until a breakdown at college led to rehab and eventually a referral to the H3 class.

'It's very vibrant,' she said cheerily, hoping to mask her dismay.

From the corner of her eye she glimpsed two class-mates – the ones Poppy referred to as Pearl and Dean – pausing to gaze at her own painting as they moved towards the layout table, bearing their own creations with all the reverence due to historic artefacts.

'Ooh, a photocopy'. This from Paul, delivered with treacly irony as he looked at Harriet's painting.

'Quite the emotional bypass.' That was Darren, his voice trilling with innuendo.

Harriet flushed, keeping her eyes glued to Poppy's painting. Then a shot of anger, as strong as anything she'd experienced in the past year, punched her stomach.

Ye gods! This was the H3 class. Health, Hope and Healing: that's what it promised to deliver. Not snide remarks or competitive angst.

Harriet turned back to her table demoralised and dejected. She could feel her spirits plunging as inexorably as water down a plughole. It was as if the life-force was draining from her body, sucking her into a vortex of misery. It felt as visceral as that agonising moment when a nurse quietly removed her stillborn baby from her arms. Grief hadn't been the emotion she'd felt then. Only this same crushing sense of despair.

Picking up her rucksack from the floor, she stowed her reference sketches and pencils in a daze. She needed to snap out of this. Why was she feeling so fragile today? Surely some silly remarks from a couple of mischief-makers shouldn't have sent her into such a tailspin.

'See you next week for the bonfire of scribbles,' said Poppy, zipping up her leather jacket as she walked past.

Harriet nodded dumbly, her thoughts elsewhere. Bonfire. That's what she needed to do with the things Ben had left behind. Burn them in the garden.

As the bus homewards lumbered fitfully across town she found herself gazing unseeingly out of the window, thinking about the past.

Oh, they'd followed all the advice thrust on them by well-meaning friends. They'd had a proper funeral for the baby; tried again. It hadn't worked. She shuddered, remembering how she'd sunk into a spiral of depression which led to increasingly bitter arguments. Time seemed to expand then contract as she looked back. Was it only ten months later that Ben hooked up with the friend of a work colleague and moved in with her? Unable to focus on anything, Harriet was signed off work by a fierce HR director and pointed in the direction of a grief counsellor. Not long after that she was made redundant from the accountancy firm where she'd worked for – what – nearly seven years? Something like that. The numbers no longer mattered. None of them.

Joining the H3 class was her counsellor's suggestion. She'd felt reluctant at first, conscious of doing nothing artistic since leaving school although she'd always enjoyed the art classes there. Then a girl-friend encouraged her to attend the initial session and she'd found Stephen Warren's promise of health, hope and healing too tantalising to ignore.

By the fifth session, though, doubts were setting in. It wasn't that she couldn't – or didn't want to – paint her emotions. It was just that her inner reality seemed to be at odds with the chaos of other people's feelings. If Lisa's sentiments were poisonous yellow and Poppy's were a psychedelic swirl of pink, blue and violent green then which colours could possibly characterise her own emotions? In her mind's eye, grief resembled an ashen fog; depression a dreary grey. She might as well paint her piece of hardboard a ghostly monotone and be done with trying to express her interior life in any hues at all.

Harriet closed her eyes tight against the intermittent sunshine and waited for an image to appear behind the lids. Out of nowhere a springtime orchard came into view. From far off, the apple blossom resembled a drifting, fair-weather cloud. Moving closer, she felt soothed by the palest of pinks and delicate, creamy whites. There were soft, yellow stamens among the petals too. Were these the shades she sought?

It was unlikely, she reflected, that Stephen Warren would appreciate such tenderness, such stillness. He was looking for drama and chaos. Raw emotion spewed across a canvas. Souls stripped bare.

Still, maybe his methods were working more subtly than she'd realised. It was a long time since she'd felt the level of anger provoked by Pearl and Dean's comments. Or perhaps the torrent of emotion had little to do with the H3 class and more to do with moving at her own pace through the seven stages of grief. Shock, denial, anger, depression – she'd endured all those emotions over the past two years. Could she dare to believe that a sense of acceptance –even hope – would come next?

Arriving home, Harriet walked along the hallway to Ben's study without bothering to remove her coat. He'd always treated the room as his personal fiefdom. For weeks after he'd gone, she'd been nervous about opening the door. It felt too intrusive somehow. As if she was breaking and entering. More recently, the grief counsellor had encouraged her to sort through the stuff he'd left behind. There were still some piles of paper to excavate but most of the books and some pictures had gone to the charity shops. Now, little remained – his desk, two chairs, a rug, empty bookshelves. It would take time to reclaim the space as her own but it was a peaceful room and north-facing with good light.

The idea came to her unbidden: it would make a perfect artist's studio.

Harriet stood in the centre of the room, her hands thrust deep in

her coat pockets, gazing at the small back garden. Spring was waking
the borders from a long winter's sleep. And there was the apple tree,
clouded with delicate pink and white blossom, just as she had
pictured on the bus. That tree was one of the reasons she resisted
moving home when Ben left. In her lowest moments she'd felt it was
her only friend.

With a flash of insight Harriet instinctively knew what she would
paint here. Not the tumultuous outpouring of emotion that excited
Stephen Warren. Nor the pallid shades of recollected grief. Just the
simple, harmonious tranquillity of nature. Trees, fields and flowers
with orderly structures and rhythmically perennial seasons from
which she and others could take quiet pleasure.

Her mind cleared as if a southerly wind had blown the clouds
away. She would sign up for that landscape painting course she'd seen
advertised in the local library. It was run by the town's adult education service so it shouldn't cost very much. Too bad if its timing
clashed with the H3 class. She doubted her sudden absence would
create much of a stir.

A tiny bubble of hope fizzed in her head as her thoughts ran on.
Building a sufficiently strong portfolio might allow her to apply for a
diploma course at art college and see where that could lead. It
wouldn't be easy but careful budgeting would mean she could live off
her redundancy money for a while yet. The idea had all the promise
of starting a fresh canvas with a clean brush.

Harriet glanced at her watch. The library would still be open if
she put on her trainers and ran all the way.

Madam I'm Adam

Eamon Somers

My creative writing tutor always says: Don't open a story with a dream, or set it in a pub. But even though I know the rules, here am I stretching my arm out to the left side of the bed. Ian is not there, the sheets are warm like he's just gone for a wee, but it has been three months.

You say: it's only been ten days, missing the point. In my dream it was three months. I'm not even in bed, I fell asleep over my pint in the Barley Mow. You hang up. Why do I bother? If I ring back, you'll say: But Ian, what about Ian? How's he doing? The question somehow planted in your mind by me, as if I'm in control. I might say: I don't really miss him, but I want to, for the validation, the confirmation that I'm a nice person. I mean he was ok and all, but what did we have in common? Not that I wanted him to be my twin. Even with newborn twins there's as much chance they'll hate each other, having to share any remaining parents, which I think is what happened to me, when you came along, and I was forced into being your fatherly big brother. How things have changed now that you treat me like I'm your baby sister.

I call you anyway: What were you doing in a pub, in the afternoon? Hopefully you've left by now, or your so-called tutor will have more words for you.

Yes, yes. I'm on my way, just passing the graveyard, next door. You know I love a funeral, people in black. Does everyone have a standby funeral outfit in their wardrobe, or do they buy one for each passing, dropped off at the charity shop after a few days to signify end of mourning, duty done?

You ignore me.

Black veils are in abundance, I say, wondering if I would be brave enough to turn up to a fancy-dress party in a black gauzy dress and equally dark veiled fascinator? I could if I was in South America for Day of the Dead. Not that you'd care, you wouldn't be there, but I value your opinion. I linger to watch the interment.

I had a letter from Ian's solicitor yesterday, urging me to put the flat on the market by the end of the month or Ian would be forced to do so. He is a drama queen, I never liked it anyway, the flat, I mean. I know you want to ask about the money, remind me that you provided half the deposit when we bought, but I mustn't encourage you. I don't know if I can bear to live here while it's on the market. Smile at potential purchasers, make up stories about why we're selling. Watch them eye up the tat, most of which belongs to him, all his art and books, and that dreadful chaise longue he covered in green material, was it brocade. I'm not sure what brocade is, shameful substandard queen that I am.

I don't know why Madam I'm Adam has come into my head. But I'm sure my writing tutor would tell me to get creative with *Adam I'm Madam*, imagine the circumstances where I would say that. Adam, the first male ever, addressing an unnamed madam, maybe Eve, or God. I whisper it, then revert to the original and say it more loudly. Madam I'm Adam. Not that I want to be Adam at a time, especially when there isn't another man in the whole world, and then to get thrown out of the Garden of Eden and be ashamed of my nakedness. Do you think God was body shaming or if it was being outside the tiny world of the Garden that brought it on?

You're silent, but I continue: poor Adam, it was just him and Eve, and God of course, retrospectively, now that the devil, not just in snake form, has been officially abolished. Eve never had a childhood and was a fully formed adult from the beginning. But they must have been in the garden for some time before the incident with the apple, which probably arose out of boredom with their perfect God-designed life. They'd never known anything except nakedness. So if God didn't put the shame on them, where did it come from?

But enough about me, what about your troubles, I say, only noticing then that you've already hung up and that I've been babbling into a listenerless phone. But I don't stop. There's a woman singing at the graveside, in a high-pitched voice, that *Carry me Over* song about Carrickfergus and Skye. It's usually sung by a man, but she's doing a lovely job. Even Ian would be impressed, although being so familiar with it, he might be affronted. Very rigid about roles, though not in our domestic arrangements, he never minded me ironing or washing dishes or taking out the bins. When I say bins... well, you know, me dropping the bag of rubbish into the chute on my way to work, at least when I was employed. But when I wasn't, oh he got quite irritable with me for taking on more domestic tasks instead of going out to look for a job. Not that jobs are found by going out anymore, it's all done online nowadays, but you know what I mean. It wasn't like I was sinking into depression; reclining on the couch watching daytime tv, property porn and quizzes, I was just filling my acknowledged voids with useful activities. Besides, it only took a couple of weeks till my writing tutor found me the opportunity of a lifetime at Brazen Books. Ian got so cross when I told him, saying it was because I don't read books, but it made me suspect he'd only gone in to flirt with the boy I replaced. And he never came to browse or flirt with me during my time there, when he could have, and without any obligation to buy a book. I mean I saved him money, or at least that boy leaving did. Saved him from adding to his shelves of dust-gathering unread books. Never any need to buy more if it wasn't the flirting that had brought him in. I'm mixing myself up now, but you know what I mean. Not that we broke up over any of this. I mean that all happened over two years ago, I've been at the dentist's for nearly a year now, and a new boy is working in Brazen Books, giving Ian all the scope in the world to resume his flirting and book buying. Unless it was me knowing things from the proprietor's side of the counter, growing into trade attitudes towards customers, and sullying his experience, introducing some sort of shame, turning his innocent indulgence into the equivalent of watching porn. Not that he'd ever shown the slightest interest in my collection.

It's weeks before you call me back. I immediately say, it's calm here today, but it will be chaos tomorrow. Ian's solicitor notified me that Ian is sending a removal team to take away his books and gewgaws. I'm intending to stay to keep an eye on the operation. Not because I care about material goods, but there are the bits and pieces you insisted I took when you were clearing out Mam's house before it went back to the council. I know they're eyeless inanimate objects, but they give off an electric resonance when I make eye contact with them. Nothing like as strong as what happens when I think of you sitting on the couch where you were conceived, making me reminisce about our childhood, fractured and all as it was. I assume Sharon is still at you to get rid of it.

Then, in the afternoon, an outfit called Domestic Goddesses is coming in to give the place 'a quick makeover' the solicitor called it, which I assume means running the vacuum over the carpets and arranging the remaining furniture and stuff in an aesthetically pleasing way, in accordance with current taste, probably different from my own. After that the photographer from the estate agents is coming round to 'populate the brochure'. There are strong hints of criticism in the solicitor's letter, how it might have been less painful if I'd organised it all when he first wrote to me. But hey I'm the grieving widow, I'm entitled to wallow. I'm taking the day off work to be here. It's costing me a day's wages. By rights I should be reimbursed.

I might be the victim, but I'm not going to be totally passive. I'll follow the photographer round and get in their shots if I don't like how things are being photographed, or arranged if the goddesses are still in attendance. I'll change everything back to how it was once they've gone. I only hope he's been honest about which chattels are going. It would have been much better if he'd begged me to let him be here to argue about what was his and what was ours and what was mine. I suppose if I really cared, that's what I'd have demanded. Please don't think I want to see him or am hoping he will come back.

You say you saw him with someone. From your description of the boy's hair and shoes I'd say it's the one from the bookshop, although perhaps there's another bloody subset of the gays I haven't heard about, and the city is teeming with lookalike boys signalling their membership, that I have been too self-absorbed to notice. I need a holiday. I'd have gone already except for the fact that I wanted to be here to make sure my interests were protected if there was a flat clearance.

Apparently he's filing for divorce. I can't imagine what the grounds are, not that it matters, it was his idea to get married, he was free to end it any time he liked, and it would have been cheaper if we hadn't been married or in a civil partnership. I never held him back. But he wanted ... well I don't know, maybe societal approval, or a replication of his own happy childhood. Apparently utterly perfect, even if you always poured scorn on the stories of his Famous Five childhood, so richly described after a voddie or two.

Remember when you talked me into therapy, and I gave up after two sessions? I talked a lot about you, asked her if your doubts about Ian were a way of disguising your attraction to him. She closed her eyes and touched her fingers together and said: isn't it equally likely your sister fancies you, that she might want some kind of triangular relationship. I just stood up and walked out. I hadn't told her about your Sharon and the two kids. I hope she stopped billing you.

I think I will have a divorce party once this chaos is out of the way and life is tidied up. You and Sharon can host it round yours if you like, provided you don't invite Ian. Or maybe Maurice could host, in his garden, a marquee erected in case it rains. You always suspected he was more than my writing tutor. He's already talking about me moving in, but I wonder if it's too soon. I mean I should be feeling some sort of grief at losing Ian after twelve happy years, wouldn't it seem a bit unseemly if I merged double quick time into Maurice's life, amended my online profile to say, 'normal service is resumed.'

I'm entitled to a period in the wilderness, a little rough sleeping maybe, time off the rails, hit rock bottom and fill everyone with concern that I might be suicidal, and then miraculously, with the guts of a year behind me, I could emerge from my miserable chrysalis and be reborn as a purer version of the princess I have always been, somehow more magnificent, more royal, more irresistible. And wouldn't it please Maurice if I got a novel out of it?

The Nearly Invisible Man

Stevyn Colgan

DCI Gavin Quisty was a character that first appeared in the novel *A Murder to Die For*. This short story is one of several that have since been written to expand upon the character.

'Draw me a bicycle.'

'Sorry?'

'Indulge me,' said Quisty. 'I want to prove a point.'

'Whatever you say,' said Woon. She produced a pen from her jacket and began scribbling on a piece of paper. Her brow furrowed.

'Having a problem there, Kim?'

'Yes, annoyingly. Why is this so hard?'

Quisty smiled and held out his smartphone. On the screen was a photo of a bicycle. Woon frowned as she compared it to her drawing.

'I was way off target. I got the frame completely wrong.'

'Don't knock yourself out about it. Most people get it wrong,' said Quisty. 'Which was entirely the point that I wanted to make. Everyone looks but very few people *see*.'

'That is such a Quisty thing to say,' said Kim Woon.

The security office was small, windowless and musty; over the past two decades a succession of security guards had eaten their take-away meals in there and the smells of Chinese five spice, fried chicken and curry powder had seeped into the plasterboard walls. Detective Sergeant Kim Woon sat at a desk that bore a multitude of coffee rings like a rusty Olympics logo. She wrinkled her nose and screwed up her abortive attempt to draw a bicycle. A bank of television monitors showed various views of the museum in real time but one was replaying CCTV footage from the previous 24 hours at double speed. During that time, someone, somehow, had done something impossible and DCI Gavin Quisty had been called in to figure out how.

The Herewardshire Hoard was discovered in a pig field near the village of Ordon in 1988 and, until 2009 and the uncovering of the Staffordshire Hoard, it had been the largest collection of Anglo-Saxon treasure ever found. It had been known for some time that a number of hoards were buried on land that was now South Here-wardshire but, to date, only one had surfaced. Or, at least, found and declared. Consisting as it did of over two hundred items, primarily made of gold and silver, the find had caused a sensation. Much of it now resided in the British Museum, partly because it was more acces-sible to the viewing public there, but mostly because of security. The County Museum at Uttercombe was small and its systems were adequate, although not extensive enough for the display of some-thing as valuable as the hoard. As the result, the museum had retained just a handful of small choice pieces made of gold: some coins, torcs and bracelets, and a few rings and necklaces. Overnight, all of it had been stolen. Which, as the museum manager had been keen to point out, was impossible.

'The museum has five rooms,' he'd explained. 'From the air the building looks like a cross or a propeller with the central hub being the Great Room in which the hoard was displayed.'

'That's the room with the big domed roof on top?' asked Woon.

'It is. The Great Room has no windows and has alarms fitted to all four of the doors that lead into it. The four rooms beyond also have alarms fitted to their doors and to their windows. There's no possible way to get into the Great Room without triggering an alarm.'

'Someone did,' said Woon.

'I can't understand it,' said the manager. 'The museum was locked up and the alarms were set. I know that for sure because I was the one who locked up. But when I opened up this morning, the hoard was gone. It's as if the items had evaporated into thin air. There were no signs of a break-in, no indications of even an attempt, and none of the alarms had been tripped. I called the police immediately, of course. The officer who came admitted that he was utterly baffled. He said it was as if we'd been robbed by a ghost. And he suggested that you have a look at it.'

'Sounds right up your street, Guv,' said Woon.

———

Quisty had begun by examining the scene of the crime. Accompanied by the museum manager and trailed by Woon, he'd moved around the room speaking into the voice recorder on his smartphone.

'On the south wall of the Great Room we have various portraits of notable historical Herewardians. I can see Elizabeth 'Big Bessie' Cockering the suffragette, and Sir Geoffrey Saltonstall, gentleman astronomer and animal husbandry enthusiast, who developed the Herewardshire Hog and funded the building of this museum. Now, moving to the—'

'Do you really need to record that level of detail?' asked Woon. 'You sound like an audio guide.'

'You know how I work, Kim. Observation is key. And doing a

running commentary encourages me to look harder for things to report. Now then ... crossing the Great Room we pass by Henry Maypie's *The Meatmen of Goyle,* a large bronze composition consisting of six life-sized figures of fat, jolly and affluent men all facing inwards in a circle as if in deep discussion. And now we arrive at the north wall where we find 18th century landscapes by Porter Angrosse, modern abstracts by Jasper Fikiss and Helena Carkington, and a portrait of an odd-looking horse by Thadeus Bultitude R.A.'

Quisty examined the door that led from the Great Room into the North Room.

'Door between the North Room and the Great Room bears a large number of scuff marks and scratches ... similar marks on architrave and chips to paintwork ...'

'Made by coat zippers and bags?' said Woon.

'Excellent,' said Quisty. 'And what else can you tell me about the marks?'

'They're lower than you'd expect them to be,' said Woon. 'So, either long coats or, most likely, people who are shorter than average. School parties I guess?'

'We don't guess, Kim. We surmise,' said Quisty. 'And I am sure that you're right. Unless this is the museum of choice for persons of restricted growth I think we can assume that school children are responsible for those marks. Children do tend to jostle more than adults. And, you'll note, the gift shop, café and exit are located in the North Room.' He returned to his narration. 'However, no evidence of the door being forced open or of hinge removal.'

'Either of which would have set off the alarm,' reiterated the manager.

'I'm being thorough,' said Quisty. 'Now, looking upwards I see no possible entry point ... no skylights or windows ... you'd be amazed Kim, just how many detectives never look up.'

'Isn't that how one of the Hoddenford bullion robbers evaded the police back in the sixties?' said the manager. 'I read that he climbed up a tree and the officers pursuing him didn't look up. They missed him, a fact that only emerged when he gloated about it on his death bed.'

'I read that too,' said Woon. 'He sat there, fifteen feet above their heads, watching everyone running about like headless chickens. He even ate his sandwiches up there. Embarrassing to say the least.'

'Well, quite,' said Quisty. 'I'm constantly surprised by how many people in general don't look up. My old art teacher used to implore us to always do so because that's where you'll find the hidden history of a building. Above the homogenous Anytown shop fronts you'll see the Gothic follies, the neo-Georgian tomfoolery, the Victorian statuary and no end of extravagant mouldings, gargoyles, grotesques and sculpted brickwork chimneys. You miss so much if you restrict your vision to eye level. I've often said that he probably taught me more about detective work than any police college ever did because he taught me to see. Not to look, but to *see*.

'That's particularly true here in the Great Room,' said the museum manager. 'The domed ceiling is painted with a precise copy of the night sky. You can't see it now but every star has been picked out in luminous paint and when we shutter the windows and switch the lights off it comes to life. It's a wonderful thing. We do it twice a day for the visitors.'

'How splendid. And speaking of wonderful things, just look at those magnificent swaggering jackasses.' He walked across to *The Meatmen of Goyle*. 'Aren't they great?'

'Pompous is the word I'd use,' said Woon.

'Which is exactly the effect that Maypie was looking to achieve,' said Quisty. 'Did you know that his work was inspired by Rodin's famous *The Burghers of Calais?*'

'I can see a similarity in the composition,' said Woon. 'But the Burghers are all skinny and dressed in rags.'

'Indeed they are,' said Quisty. 'As I'm sure you know, Rodin's sculpture commemorates the heroism of six French notables who, in order to save the port of Calais, were willing to surrender their lives. They'd held out for a year against the English invaders – this was during the Hundred Years War – but they eventually ran out of food and water. The price that King Edward III demanded for ending the siege was the lives of six prominent citizens. They promptly volunteered and were ordered to walk out of Calais wearing nooses around their necks and carrying the keys to the city. They were willing to die for their people. This so impressed King Ted that he spared their lives and their heroism has never been forgotten.'

'It's a great story, although probably apocryphal,' added the manager 'It was certainly enough to inspire Rodin. And he, in turn, inspired Maypie. However, in stark contrast, this sculpture is all about boasting and self-congratulation.'

'So it's a parody of the Burghers?' asked Woon.

'Indeed it is,' said the manager, pleased to have an opportunity to show off his own knowledge. '*Meatmen* was sculpted just two years after Rodin's figures went on display and follows his plan of six individual figures arranged in a tableau and sufficiently spaced apart so that everyday folk can walk in and around them. The genius of Maypie's work is the contrast between Rodin's gaunt, heroic, self-sacrificing burghers and our plump, overstuffed South Herewardshire meat growers. These were the men who ran the stock yards and markets at Goyle and they represented the wealth of the county, which, in Regency times, was the richest county in Great Britain. We were known as the meat locker of England you know. It's a glorious work of social satire.'

'And the best thing of all is that the men who commissioned the artwork knew nothing of Rodin and had no idea that Maypie was making fun of them,' said Quisty. 'Isn't that joyous?'

'That's all well and good,' said Woon. 'But if you're going to let the public wander around among these porkers, you should clean them better.' She held out her hand to show a large golden-brown smudge across her palm. It glittered like metallic paint. 'I don't know if this is polish, Marmite or the result of a dirty protest but, whatever it is, if that had got on my suede jacket I'd be livid.'

Quisty took hold of her hand and bowed his head to smell it.

'Now, that's interesting,' he said, sniffing. 'That's very interesting.'

Woon had a tentative smell for herself.

'Waxy,' she said. 'Or greasy. Like a candle.'

'I do apologise,' said the manager. 'The bronzes are coated to protect them. A professional firm comes in to do it. Nothing should ever rub off on a visitor.'

'I don't imagine for a second that you're to blame,' said Quisty. 'And I'm pretty sure that I now know how your ghost was able to steal the hoard.'

After he had completed his investigative tour of the Great Room, Quisty had asked to see the CCTV recordings. Frustratingly, the museum wasn't internally lit at night so as soon as it had closed its doors for the evening, the Great Room had been plunged into darkness. Nothing showed on the screen except silent, impenetrable blackness. There was no audio to the recording either.

'It's like that for the whole night. Whoever committed the crime did so in complete darkness,' explained the manager.

'Not so difficult to do if you're a frequent visitor to the museum and know the layout,' said Quisty.

'Like a member of staff?' asked Woon.

'Definitely not,' said the manager. 'We have a small staff and I know them all extremely well. None of them would have done this.'

'I'm quite sure of that,' said Quisty. 'There's something else going on here. Something we're not seeing.'

For a further hour, Quisty watched the CCTV footage. He fast-forwarded through the eight hours of darkness and watched as the manager opened up, switched on the lights and discovered the theft. He saw police officers come and go and conduct their investigation. And then the public were let back inside. Visitors came and went, singly and in groups, all moving about the Great Room and nearly all stopping to look at the scene of the crime.

'What are you hoping to see?' said Woon. 'The theft happened overnight.'

'I have an idea,' said Quisty. 'And I just need one more connection, one more fact to give the idea veracity.'

Suddenly a curator entered the room and appeared to be asking for everyone's attention. The screen went black.

'What's happened?' said Woon.

'That's the morning blackout,' said the museum manager. 'We have two every day at 11am and 3pm. It's when we show off Sir Geoffrey Saltonstall's planetarium.'

'Ah, the painted ceiling,' said Woon.

'Yes. It takes a few seconds for people's eyes to adjust but once they do it's like looking into the clearest night sky you've ever seen,' said the manager. 'It's one of the museum's most popular attractions even though it only lasts for about quarter of an hour. Health and Safety won't let us do it for any longer. It has to be a complete blackout to work, and as they're all standing, there's the potential for trips and falls. If people were seated it might be different.'

On the screen, the lights came back on and people rubbed their aching eyes as they made the transition back to light.

'Aha!' said Quisty. He sat back triumphantly in his chair. 'Were I a boastful man, I'd shout 'Eureka!' right now and run naked down the street.'

'What?' said Woon.

'Look closely at the screen,' said Quisty. 'What can you see?'

'I see people mooching about in the Great Room letting their eyes adjust,' said Woon.

'You're looking but you're not seeing,' said Quisty.

'What's the difference?' asked Woon.

'Draw me a bicycle,' said Quisty.

Later that evening, and back in the CID office at Uttercombe, Kim Woon reflected upon the day.

'I now understand what you said about learning more from your art teacher than from the police,' said Woon. 'I still can't believe that I didn't spot it.'

'It's not your fault,' said Quisty. 'You're at the mercy of your own brain. It may be the most powerful processing engine in the known universe, handling something like four hundred billion bits of information every second, but it doesn't have unlimited capacity. We experience everything we are exposed to but we are only really conscious of around 2000 bits of data per second because, quite unconsciously, our brains filter out most of the noise. It has to make some sort of order from the chaos. And it's a good thing it does or we'd all go bonkers from sensory-overload. Our brains also take shortcuts by creating snapshots; very basic impressions of what things look like for comparison and recognition purposes. So, for example, if I ask you to visualise a bicycle, you can do that easily because your memory holds a snapshot based upon all the bicycles you've ever seen. So, if I ask you to draw a bicycle, what happens? Things go horribly wrong is what happens. What shape is the frame? How do the pedals and gears work? What's the pattern of spoking on the wheels? You may have a snapshot of a bicycle in your mind but it's very basic and low res. It's missing the fine detail, which is why you can't draw one. The ability to represent something reasonably accurately as a work of art requires you to examine a bicycle closely to understand how it all fits together. It's why I do a commentary when examining a crime scene – it forces me to see rather than look.'

'Which is why I didn't see the extra Meatman,' said Woon.

'Exactly,' said Quisty. 'You were concentrating so hard on looking for a suspect among the visitors that you let your mental snapshot of the sculpture override your ability to see it properly.'

'It's ridiculous,' said Woon. 'I know that the sculpture has six figures. I walked all around the bloody thing yesterday. So why didn't I notice that there were seven Meatmen on the CCTV footage?'

'There's an amazing experiment – you may have seen it – where a researcher asks a subject to watch a short video clip of a basketball player and to count how many times the player scores,' said Quisty. 'Afterwards they ask the subject for an answer and it's generally correct. They then ask, 'Did you spot the gorilla?' After some confusion, the researcher replays the same piece of video and, sure enough, about halfway through, a guy in a gorilla suit walks across the screen from left to right and even waves at the camera. But 90% of subjects never see the gorilla. Their brains filter it out so that they can concentrate on counting the basketball dunks.'

'I bet you'd spot the gorilla wouldn't you?' said Woon.

'Only because I've taught myself to see.'

'Which is how you spotted the extra Meatman.'

'To be fair, I did get a nudge about what to look for from that greasy mark on your hand,' said Quisty. 'That was an important clue.'

'It was?'

'Have you never trod the boards, Kim? Did you never strut and fret your hour upon the stage?'

'I was always more of a sports girl.'

'Shame. If you had then you'd know the smell of greasepaint,' said Quisty. 'And bronze-coloured greasepaint immediately made me think of those living statues you see on the High Street. After that it was simple to put two and two together. Except I couldn't. Not quite. There was an important piece of the jigsaw missing. Namely, how did the suspect change out of his living statue costume and back again without being seen?'

'The blackouts.'

'Exactly. I now know that he made a series of visits to learn the layout of the museum. On his last two visits he posed as a blind man and did the whole thing with his eyes shut, just to prove to himself that he could move around in complete darkness, essential to avoid being caught on CCTV. He then made up a reversible set of clothes for the quick change and he was ready to go.'

'So he came into the museum as a visitor and waited for the 3pm blackout. He then changed in the dark, slathered his face in bronze greasepaint – getting some on the statues by accident – and then, when the lights came back on he was a seventh Meatman,' said Woon. 'No one noticed because their eyes were adjusting and because it didn't even occur to them to check how many sculptures there were.'

'And with most of the visitors being children with no interest in anything other than the gift shop and having a milk shake in the café, he was invisible to them,' said Quisty. 'He was the gorilla. All he had to do was stand still and wait until closing time, something he'd trained himself to do for hours on end. He then committed the theft at night and stashed the loot inside his padded costume. Come the morning, he was back in position for opening time. He knew that, during the distraction caused by the theft, no one would notice an extra Meatman. Then, a couple of hours of standing still later, he used the 11am blackout to remove his greasepaint and turn his clothes outside in. Then he joined the museum visitors unnoticed and walked out in plain sight. Quite brilliant.'

'And lucky that the museum didn't cancel the morning blackout. He'd have had to stand there until 3pm.'

'He was audacious, I'll give him that. But he obviously thought it was worth the risk and, with so many school parties booked to come in, it was pretty likely that the blackouts would go ahead. After all, they only last for fifteen minutes or so.'

'And, as he was one of only four human statues in the borough, it wasn't so hard to track him down and arrest him. He probably thought that no one would guess how he did it.'

'Not guess. Surmise,' said Quisty. 'Ratiocination, not conjecture. You know what? You should take up drawing as a hobby, Kim. It trains the eye to see and focuses the mind. It teaches you to see past the superficial.'

'Me? All I can draw is stick men.'

'Don't put yourself down,' said Quisty. 'Things worked out pretty well for Mr Lowry.'

SANCTUARY

PETE LANGMAN

'It's you. You're the one ... you're the one.'

I'm in my usual spot at the Mucky Duck, squeezed into a corner between the disabled toilet and the exit to the beer garden. On the table in front of me the barest stub of a candle flickers in the neck of an old Jack Daniel's bottle. Its flaming heart sends fresh drips sliding down to join the great gouts of the once-molten material now frozen to the bottle's sides, obscuring the label. They are wallflowers of wax, destined to forever haunt the shadowlands of the party's periphery. But there is no party. There's only me. Me and a pint of IPA. Its creamy head, barely an inch below the rim, caresses the edges of the waxy pink crescent moon that adheres to the smeared translucence of the glass. It is neither my colour nor my lipstick. Across the room my reflection stares out from the pub's blackened window, expressionless. Silent. My phone, a slab of inconsiderate animation in this *Still Life with Girl* (2023), flashes out text after text:

Are you ok?

I love you.

Call me.

But I no longer see this. Pint, glass, lipstick: all are forgotten. Instead, I stare at the blister pack that lies beside the distressed bottle of Jack. Just a single dome remains intact, the final scene in the third and final act.

The Mucky Duck. It's an appropriate venue, at least. I've been coming here since I was barely fifteen and it was the Rose and Crown. Snakebite and black for lasses and happy hour all night every night because my boyfriend worked behind the bar. I practically grew up in this pub – it was certainly where I cast off the shackles of childhood. I had my first real drink here. I lost my virginity here, just over there where the fruit machine now loiters like an ambitious extra in a B-movie trying just a little too hard to catch the director's eye. And it was here that my father explained it to me. My mother's death, that is, and how I, how ... how I might be more like her than I knew. It was here that I opened the letter that told me exactly how like her I was.

Back then, the Rose and Crown was my place, my turf. It always allowed me to be. It wasn't a place to hide, it wasn't somewhere the real world couldn't reach me. It was the real world. When I walked through the front door the shackles fell away. But that world changed. That letter changed everything.

I ran. To university. To London. To my career. I left the world of the Rose and Crown behind. I meant never to return.

But my father's days down the pit finally caught up with his lungs, and while the stubborn bastard held onto life like grim death, his last year and a half broke us both. By the time his body accepted that it could hold on no longer I'd been nursing it for months – dad had long since vanished, as had my job in the big smoke, along with the obligatory Docklands flat and the Chelsea Harbour boyfriend.

By then the Rose and Crown had turned into this, the Mucky Duck, a pub with ideas below its station. My den of iniquity had grown up. I had grown up. I used to sneak out of my parents' house to rebel quietly in the corner with roll-ups and sticky pints, but no longer. The house was mine, and it was the pub quiz that drew me out. First Tuesday of every month. I was here just twenty-three days ago, arguing with Midge and my date over the answers. I had abandoned any pretence that I wasn't turning into my mother. I had long since turned.

The argument was pointless. Two boys who knew bugger all about football and even less about philosophy. It was hardly fair. Sartre, you idiots. Busby indeed.

I sent my date to the bar to get a round plus shots, because it was time. Time for pill no. 6. But Midge, bless him, Midge refused to let me take it. Midge who should have known better. Midge who I met at Uni, where we went from being the 'couple most likely' directly to 'just great friends' in a few short weeks, totally skipping the boyfriend/girlfriend bit. I mean, we did try friends with benefits but it just wasn't us. It was as if we were too in tune to let things get out of hand. Too close to go one step beyond. It just seemed ... silly.

I had barely taken the strip out of my bag when he just said 'no.' Just like that. No. As if.

Well, I said, I don't need your permission. Look at me, I said. Look at the state I'm in. You know the prognosis. Like your mother, he said. Like my mother, I said. He came back at me with the old standby, 'cross that bridge when you come to it,' and I pointed out that when I came to that particular bridge it would be because I could no longer cross it alone. He'd either have to carry me across or watch me choke to death on my own saliva while sitting in a pool of my own piss.

Perhaps he'd prefer that.

Ok, that's a little unfair, and maybe he would hold my hand as I slipped away and maybe everyone would say 'how compassionate, what a true friend', but where's my dignity? Where's my choice?

Well, my choice is here, I told him. My choice is now. I choose this.

He told me he loved me and he couldn't let me do it and I said if he did love me he'd not only let me he'd make sure I did. If he loved me he'd see that my body doesn't just disobey me, it denies me. It denies my even being me. I say I am not this disease, but this body – my body – says different. I look in the mirror and see someone else, someone I refuse to be. I am not what I am.

Poor monster. There's probably a term for it, this seething ball of auto-alienation.

I did not ask for this.

I did not ask for his love.

Midge just necked his pint and walked out. Bastard. Some friend he turned out to be. He left me behind with this pretty but dim boy. My Tinder pick for the evening. Poor lad, having to watch me and Midge argue. He was already confused enough, being on a tag-along date with this weird girl in a chair and her not-boyfriend who was visiting from out of town. I explained to him how I wanted to go: unexpectedly, in my sleep. I mean, who wouldn't? I told him I'd taken the plunge, signed the disclaimer. They gave me a strip of thirty pills. I was to take one at 10 every evening. The pills had a coating that dissolved in six hours. One of the thirty was fatal. This exotic version of Russian roulette meant that I would go to sleep each night not knowing if I'd wake. I would spend every night as if it were my last, because it might just be that. I could surround myself with friends, whatever I wanted, whatever meant I could lay my head on my pillow and think to myself yes, I am content: now would be just fine. Even if that was just quiz night at the Mucky Duck.

He didn't really get it. I didn't really expect him to. But then again, I hadn't swiped right to have an in-depth discussion of ethics. I asked him to take me home and fuck me instead, but I guess the 4% chance of it being my last ever fuck was too much pressure. Boys, eh? What does a girl have to do?

Midge returned as unexpectedly as he'd left. He stood behind my wheelchair, wrapped his arms around me and kissed me on the ear. He told my date that he'd made the right decision, that he wasn't missing anything. Told him I was a lousy shag. Told him he'd only come back to make sure I took the pill. Then we played pool. Just like old times. Just Midge and me. Old times.

That was 23 nights ago. Since then? Well, it makes no odds. Now is all that matters. And now I'm alone at my table, someone else's lipstick on my glass, staring at this, my last pill: the one. So much for the unexpected. I hadn't considered this possibility. This was not what I agreed. The point was that I wouldn't know. But it turns out I do.

Just my bloody luck.

Cowboy time, we used to call it. Ten minutes to ten. Ten minutes before ... you.

I signed the consent forms. The convoluted disclaimers. I honestly think they'd sue me if I didn't finish the course. You know, like antibiotics. If you don't finish the course you put everyone's health in danger. And if you do ...

But with this lot, it's different. The last pill you take finishes the course. You don't expect the course to finish with the last pill.

And as for the last breakfast of a condemned woman, I ate my 30th this morning.

This place. This place was always where I came when I needed simply to be.

And this is the place where I now sit, staring at my nemesis. This nemesis that is my sanctuary from myself.

Ironic, really.

FINAL FLING

VIRGINIA MOFFATT

Love, so they say, changes everything.

For Tim Forsyth, the timing couldn't be worse. He is not looking for love, he is looking for a First. Not any old First either; no, he wants to get the highest Economics mark the university has ever seen. He aims to be the leading Economist of his generation, to create a twenty-first century approach to the subject, one that defeats capitalism, changes the world and enables him to win the Nobel Prize. He has a schedule to keep up. He simply doesn't have time for love.

Tonight though, he has let Ed drag him away from his textbooks to a party at the Final Fling, the oldest bar on campus. By day, a café of dubious reputation; at night, cheap alcohol is served, and the tables are pushed back to reveal a wooden dance floor that had been trampled on by generations of students. For one last night before revision starts in earnest, people are determined to party hard. They huddle together round tables littered with empty beer glasses and bottles of cider. Couples fondle in corners. The dance-floor is crowded, the music is thumping, the room is hot and stinks of sweat.

He notices her as he reaches the bar. She is a few places down, giving her order to the barman. She is dressed simply in hipster jeans, a blue camisole and a white wrap-over shirt on top. As she leans forward, he catches a tantalising glimpse of breast. She has a heart-shaped face, and a soft mouth; her dark brown hair is tied in loose plaits. He watches entranced till the order is complete, she picks up her drinks and floats back to her table. She serves her friends and sits down. Tim can't take his eyes off her.

'Wow.' Tim turns to Ed.

'She's fit all right.'

'I saw her first.'

'I'm sort of taken at the moment. She's all yours.'

Drinks purchased, Tim wanders over to her table, leaning forward with a smile, 'I bet you look good on the dance floor.'

'Of course I do,' she says, smiling as he walks away. Her flatmate Siobhan rolls her eyes, 'Where did he come from? The noughties?'

'He's got a nice smile,' she replies, 'And he dresses well.' She appraises him from afar. In his crisp white shirt and tight blue jeans he looks like he's stepped out of a frat boy movie. He's cute, she thinks, though Kaz Whiting is not looking for love either. She aims to enjoy life, wherever she is. When she is done here, she is going to go round the world. Love would interfere with her travel plans: she simply doesn't have the time. But... he has a look about him that is rather tempting. And... it's been a while.

'He's a bit *too* good looking, don't you think?' asks Siobhan.

'Naa,' Kaz runs her eyes up and down his body. Muscles, but not too muscly, slim but not too slim, 'He'll do nicely tonight.'

'Kaz!!' the table laughs in outrage.

The girls get up to dance. The music is playing a loud repetitive beat. Kaz loses herself to the rhythm. She moves her body in one fluid motion: she is dancing for the handsome boy. She unties her wrap around shirt and slips it down her arms, well aware that her camisole top accentuates her cleavage: she moves closer so that he can almost touch her. He sits forward, unable to look away, giving her time to study his eyes (beautiful), nose (perfect shape) and lips (oh-so-kiss-able). She smiles and turns back towards her friends, twisting her bottom and lowering her shirt down her back conscious of his gaze behind her. She gyrates to the increasing tempo, the shirt falling off the end of her arms. As the music reaches a crescendo, she turns back to face him, pulls off the shirt and throws it on the floor. He stares at her intently. Sweat rolls down her back, and trickles down her nose. She picks up her shirt, drapes it over her bare shoulder and saunters towards him.

'Coming then?'

'Where?'

'My place, of course.'

I can afford one night, he thinks, just one. He follows her out of the bar.

Though Kaz's place is a short walk away, they are so busy kissing it takes them half an hour to arrive. Normally, he'd be disturbed by the piles of dirty plates in the kitchen, the half full ashtrays, the unwashed clothes in her bedroom and the lingering smell of weed. But tonight, desire trumps disgust; that, and the thought that it's only one night. He can tolerate any kind of mess for this one night with her. And it was worth it, he thinks as he drifts off to sleep, for this one last bit of fun.

Morning brings the hangover from hell, punctuated by the stink of sweaty clothes and cigarette smoke. She still looks beautiful sleeping amid the smell and dirt, but he can't wait to get away. And yet, after a day's hard slog in the library, made even harder by the lack of sleep, he finds he cannot stop thinking about her. At ten he texts to discover she is feeling the same. This time they meet near his place, for a drink that quickly turns into a snog and an even more rapid departure back home.

· · ·

Normally, she'd be disturbed by the perfection of his house, the spotless kitchen, the bedroom with nothing out of place except for his running kit, the laundry piled neatly in the washing basket. But, on this occasion, Kaz finds desire trumps distaste; that, and the thought that there's no way this is going to last. She can tolerate this sterile suffocating space to enjoy this night with him.

Morning brings a different experience. She wakes to find him gone for a run, leaving her in a room so tidy, she dare not move in case she displaces something. A faint smell of bleach lingers in the air. This place will kill her if she has to stay any longer. He's gorgeous, but... she can't wait to get away.

Despite their intentions, to their surprise they find they can't stop there. They keep coming back for more, even though their time together is brief. They are creatures of the night: tangled limbs locked in wordless embraces that end too soon. They part reluctantly at dawn, forced apart by the drumbeat of revision that even Kaz can't escape, promising to see each other later.

Daylight brings frustrations. They meet for brief lunches, crammed between the endless hours of study. They find these encounters increasingly unsatisfying.

'Why do you smoke weed?' he asks. 'It's a disgusting habit.'

'It helps me relax,' she says, 'You should try it. Would do wonders for your exam tension.'

He shakes his head, and wonders whether she is too much of a distraction. And the state of her house! How can he be with someone who lives in such squalor? Then she stands up to leave; he glimpses her marvellous curves and his doubts disappear.

'Why do you have to run every morning?' she asks, 'Can't you stay in bed with me a little longer?'

'It helps me relax,' he says, 'You should try it. Would do wonders for your exam tension.'

She snorts with laughter and wonders why they are together. He seems a little... well... driven. And the state of his house! How can she be with someone who lives in such perfection? Then he smiles at her with those blue eyes and her reservations vanish.

Lying in bed, they decide the problem is not their differences. It is simply that they don't have enough time together. What they need, they decide, is a something to look forward to. Wouldn't it be brilliant to escape on holiday when exams are done? They sneak away from studying to browse vacations, dreaming of just the two of them, no distractions, undiluted love. It is Tim who suggests a barge holiday.

Just the thing, thinks Kaz. We'll snuggle up cozy at night, rise late, meander down river from pub to pub.

Can't wait, thinks Tim. We'll plan a route, do ten miles a day, get round the whole circuit in a week. It'll be great.

How they long for that time to come.

The exams end in a blaze of celebratory sunshine. They part company for a while, visiting family and friends. Their next meeting will be at the boat-yard. They cannot wait.

Creatures of the night, how will they fare by day?

Tim sees her first, his spirits rising at the sight of her. They hug and he smells the cannabis in her hair. He hates that about her. For a moment

he wonders if this is such a good idea. Kaz grasps his hand, dragging
him onto the deck of the narrow-boat and his spirits rise again. They
go down below to explore the living quarters. The roof is low, Tim
bangs his head and curses. They squeeze through the thin corridor
into a small sitting room, two benches with drawers underneath and
pink cushions on top. Beyond this is a tiny toilet and shower room, a
double bed with lurid purple bedspread, and a minute kitchen.

'Small is beautiful,' he says, 'So are you.' He pulls her towards
him. They fall on the bed together laughing.

'That was lovely,' says Kaz afterwards, thinking how nice it would
be to linger here for once. But Tim is up almost immediately, pulling
maps from his kagoul, planning a frightening looking schedule. She
wonders for a moment if this is such a good idea, but then she is
caught up in his enthusiasm. She, too, is eager to get on with it.

The first few miles of their journey take them through the
outskirts of the city. It is not a pretty sight. The footpath is covered
with nettles, littered with shopping trolleys, rusty bicycles and broken
glass. The canal runs through an industrial estate, disused red brick
warehouses, a scrap yard, a large car park. The water is rank and
black, their prow forcing its way as if through treacle. Rain begins to
fall softly. They make slow progress till the city is eventually left
behind. A field of red poppies blazes beside them, but they barely
notice it. All they are conscious of is grey rain and the smell of
manure; even the cows look miserable. Their clothes begin to get
damp. Water trickles down Kaz's nose and the back of Tim's neck.
This is not quite what they had in mind.

Tim quickly takes control, planning early starts, thrilling to each
milestone passed and pushing on far into the evening. Kaz stands at
the wheel, resentful that she has been denied another lie in to stand
here in the pouring rain. Water trickles down her nose again, this is
not quite what she had in mind. By Monday, she is in a state of rebel-
lion. She refuses to get up and they are late getting away. When they
finally get going, Tim is fretful as he steers through the rain. Water

keeps trickling down the back of his neck, this is not quite what he had in mind.

Sometimes, when Kaz is steering, Tim goes for a run. She watches him disappear up the towpath in the driving rain and feels deserted. When he returns, he laughs at her for being a slowcoach: a joke she doesn't appreciate. When Tim is steering, Kaz often takes herself downstairs. She rolls herself spliffs that leave the cabin rich in aromatic smoke. If he comes below, the smell irritates him, and the mess she has scattered about her, irritates him even more. He returns to the surface, impatient to breathe clean air.

The narrow-boat fills with steaming wet clothes that are never quite dry. The windows condense constantly. Below deck they get in each other's way. Even the bed feels crowded. They begin to argue about everything.

How they long for the holiday to end.

On the penultimate day of their holiday, their results are due. The rain stops and allows a watery sun to come out, as they go to the pub to check their academic records. Their simultaneous cries ring round the garden,

'I don't believe it!'

Kaz knows a 2:1 is more than she deserves. She skips about, shrieking out loud.

Tim sits with his head in his hands. After all his hard work, he's left with a 2:1. He deserves more than this.

'What's the matter?' she says.

'It's the end of everything.'

'Lighten up. It's just an exam. Come on share a spliff with me to celebrate.'

Now she is laughing at him. It's all her fault. If she hadn't come along entrancing him with her body, he'd have done it. Suddenly he has had enough. He marches back to the narrow-boat and collects her stash, cigarette papers, lighters, hash. He throws the lot overboard. She watches as they float away in the current.

'Why did you do that?'

'I've blown my career, thanks to you.'

She looks at him as if seeing him for the first time. He's so fucking uptight. That cannabis cost her a lot of money too. Well two can play at that game, she thinks. She dives below and returns with his running kit. Before he can stop her, she is throwing things in the water: one final fling, and the trainers sink with a loud plop.

'You silly bitch, they're worth a lot of money.'

'This was supposed to be a holiday, not an endurance test.'

She storms off. It has started raining again. He thinks, sod it, I'll moor here for the rest of the day.

She'll be back.

She does not return.

She walks across the fields shaking with rage and tears. The rain soaks her. He'll follow her, surely he will.

He doesn't.

She hits a road, stands there with her thumb up. A passing motorist takes pity on her, and drives her to the nearest town.

When love ends, life resumes.

.   .   .

He finds solace in the salary a merchant bank offers. By Christmas, he has enough to buy a flat in London's Docklands and decides the world doesn't need saving after all. She works two jobs to raise money for her trip. In April, she boards a plane for America. A life of adventure awaits.

Time passes. And love comes calling again.

Kaz literally runs into Bob at Golden Gate Park. When they catch their breath, they like what they see.

'Been running long?' he asks her later.

'Only since I've been travelling. My ex used to run and it drove me nuts. Now I find I can't get enough. Funny, isn't it?' He smiles at her and she thinks *it's been a while, he'll do nicely.*

Tim meets Susie at Ed's birthday party. She is plump, blonde and beautiful. Above the noise of the music, he shouts, 'My, you've got curves in all the right places.'

She laughs, and beckons him to sit down. They start to talk. Presently she fumbles in her bag, drawing out cigarette papers and some dope. 'Want some?'

He hesitates, then thinks, why the hell not? 'Alright, then. Thanks.'

He takes a drag of the sweet-smelling cigarette, puts his arm round her. Ed winks at him, and he winks back.

Love changes everything.

FOR THE SAKE OF SKY

MILES M HUDSON

The Welsh Dragons stormed the village on a cold February night, with screaming and gruff shouts. Tony Hightower ran outside with his father, and both were immediately blinded by the darkness. The crescent moon had set before midnight, and by 2038, there had been no street lighting for ten years.

They heard smashing doors and more shouting, as nearby bandits instructed their victims that even the slightest resistance would be met with extreme violence. Not just a mild beating to overcome those who would protect their provisions: these raiders killed with machetes and axes.

Nobody had made it to the Hightower's cottage yet. 'I'll go and look after Nan,' they heard Sky shout from behind.

Tony idolised his big sister but was concerned about her out in the darkness on her own, no matter how well she knew the territory. He turned back to her on the threshold of their home.

'You can't go over there alone, Sky. It's too dangerous. This raid sounds worse than ever.'

She waved her hand in disdain. 'I have to, even if they don't attack Nan's place, she'll be scared.' Pulling up the zip on her padded jacket, Sky was now sealed into a concealing outfit. A black beanie hat hid her blonde hair so only her pale face would shine out in the dark night.

'But remember the buddy system.' Tony's imploring was almost a whine. 'You can't go alone.' He gestured towards where their father – his battle buddy – stood waiting for Tony to join him on the path around their leather tanning yard. Dan Hightower was clearly agitated by the delay and signalled to his son to hurry up.

'Nan's my buddy. We'll be safe together.' She scowled at him, ready to defy the village's defence rules. 'I can't believe we're still having these raids. I told the village meeting six months ago we should install the audiopts system!'

'They're old, Sky, they don't understand that nothing can take us back to how it was before the Times of Malthus.'

'But it's so frustrating! We've got a surveillance system that can tell us where anybody is and what they're doing, and it's already installed, on all the network towers and everyone's Armulet.' She waved her left forearm, highlighting the smart device that clung around the sleeve of her coat, secure inside the leather holder their father had made. 'With their auditory and optic nerve signals intercepted remotely, raiders like these could never get near us by surprise – unless they came wearing blindfolds and earplugs!'

'I know, I hear you, but it's not up and running, so all we can do is protect ourselves tonight. We'll hassle for another village vote, you'll get through to them next time with just a bit more of your usual charm and persuasion, especially after this!'

'I don't know. I tried to tell them months ago but no. "All-pervasive surveillance is not for us," they said. They're good people, Tony, but they just don't get it.'

Tony was getting anxious. The debate was delaying his deployment to guard Highnam's winter grain store with their father. Despite Sky being five years older, Tony always felt he should protect her. He knew she was as strong and capable as he was, if not more so, but the instinct to guard his sibling ran deep.

She was seething. 'Nobody better die tonight, because of a few outdated ideas.' She pulled the door closed behind her and set off silently towards the deeper part of the woods and their grandmother's little house.

Tony watched his beloved sister prepare to steal away into the shadows. As crashing noises were carried to him on the wind, his fear for her was profound. He begged her: 'Call us when you get there.'

She would not call. The defence protocols included keeping their Armulet channels free for emergency redeployment instructions. This was a rule he knew she wouldn't see the need to break. As always, she would have immediately set her Armulet to video record everything in front of her on being awoken. Sky was a natural to follow in her father's footsteps, as head of Highnam's security.

As she headed into the wooded gloom, Tony could see her mutter something into her Armulet. Something about 'Record... Highnam... audiopts' but he couldn't make it out and there was no time to waste as he joined his father.

Dan and Tony illuminated their immediate area with the Armulets' glowlamp function and moved on swiftly. At the grain storehouse they encountered only one raider trying to carry off a sack of barley and he was soon sent packing, though the Highnam approach was considerably more restrained than the Welsh Dragons. Dan hit the man on the side of the head with a cricket bat then allowed him to stagger away into the chill of the night.

Tony stepped after, with an old wheel brace, raised to strike, but a hand grabbed his wrist. 'Enough. That man will have a family too.'

'But he'll just go to another house and set upon somebody there.'

Dan shook his head, wiped sweat from his forehead and thick grey beard. 'Violence can only beget more violence. We know our role for attacks like this.' He pointed back at the farm shed. 'Circle round and make sure it's all secure.'

Tony dutifully followed the plan for their station. After a lap of the small barn, he took up position at the opposite corner from his father. They couldn't see each other, but between them could watch all four sides of the building.

It was cold enough for Tony to jump up and down on the spot and flap his arms to keep warm, as the wind ruffled his hat and swirled unclear noises about his ears that he strained to hear.

In the inky dark, he could make out only shouts or crashes from elsewhere in the village. When the intervals between each noise drew out, his imagination ran riot.

With radio silence, his father was the only person Tony knew to be safe. He would hear any action on the other side of the shed, but about everyone else in Highnam, he could only wonder.

I hope mother's safe. Tony thought about his beloved family. His mother was a stout woman, physically forceful, in contrast to her daughter, who was slender, almost waif-like. Sky's strength came through her natural ability to engage, motivate and influence others.

Sky could find out what people thought about anything and everything. She would question them in gentle, friendly, happy interrogations that drew forth so much, even information someone might not have been aware they had to share.

Where was she? What was happening elsewhere? Tony ached to call Sky on the Armulet – she always had news. At the very least she could confirm whether their grandmother was protected. He hoped that an old woman hiding in her bed would never attract aggression, but this raid seemed different. It was more chaotic, sounded more violent. He was desperate for any report.

The blackness was a strait jacket around him, an endless vacuum of waiting. Dan had once told him of the visions that might visit sentries in the night and now, every rustle in the bushes, every shadow moved by the wind in the trees, every cry from a distance, became a bandit ready to charge at Tony with an axe.

Eventually, the horizon began to brighten. No raiders had returned to the grain store and by the relief of dawn, it remained unplundered. But they soon learned this was a cruel and hollow victory.

Ten residents had been killed. And the unthinkable... Sky was missing.

The ban on calls was lifted but she wasn't answering. Tony used the locator to track his sister's device and was first to the spot it indicated. She was not there. He felt everything draining from him. He banged the screen and shouted at the machine on his wrist, 'Find Sky!' It flashed up the exact place where he was standing.

Father and son combed the area, eventually finding her Armulet in its embroidered leather holder. Both buckles had been ripped off as the object had clearly been torn from her slim forearm.

After three hours of searching, her body was found in the woods about a mile out of Highnam. Dan and Amanda Hightower, rushed to their daughter's lifeless form.

She had been cut in several places, and her clothing was tattered. That beautiful face, which could so easily have graced the small screen in the old days, was slashed and broken.

When they returned, Tony, as instructed, was waiting in the threshold of their empty home – the last place he had seen his sister alive. 'Where is she?' His parents' faces were ashen, frozen, like plastic masks.

Amanda shook her head and pushed past him, heading straight upstairs.

Dan put a hand on his son's shoulder and spoke quietly, towards the ground, as if to himself. 'They took her to Highnam Court's old cellar. It's the only place we could keep so many bodies till we can bury them all.'

Tony stared at their backs as his father followed his mother up the stairs. Nothing more was said. He collapsed against the door jamb. The worst of his imaginings had precipitated from vapour into reality. Sky was gone.

A seemingly endless week later, Tony stamped around the workshop. Every response was either a shout or an object banged down. His anger at his father had grown to a rage that would not be contained. His every utterance was argumentative, gainsaying, contrariness without foundation.

As well as being the local tanner and leatherworker, his father oversaw Highnam's security. Every strategy for their village's safety had been created by Dan Hightower. His maps and plans for their defence had hung for years in the orangery at the old manor house, now the community's meeting place.

They had followed all his instructions, reinforcing buildings, blocking woodland paths with thick hedging or fences. They'd even destroyed Brunel's old stone bridge over the upper reaches of the river Severn to restrict entry to Highnam.

Every household had been equipped with low-key weaponry, designed to avoid escalating any violence. The gruff tones of his father resounded heavily in Tony's mind: 'If you bring a gun to a knife fight, you immediately turn it into a gunfight.'

Tony punched the wall. He was furious with his father, but not only for his mistakes. Yes, the hero of his first sixteen years was no longer infallible. Yes, his father's blinkered view of where an attack would come from had overlooked the possibility of raiders approaching from the west, through the Forest of Dean. Ignoring that had, in Tony's mind, directly led to Sky's murder, but even this, Tony could have forgiven.

No, this implacable rage had been fired by his father's inexplicable response to his sister's death. Over these terrible days, Dan had merely wandered zombie-like through the day, talking pragmatically about the next batch of leather to be tanned, the goatskins to be washed, the food to be cooked.

The man didn't even mention Sky. Tony struggled to process her death, yes, but his father's silence about the agonising loss of his treasured sibling only rubbed salt into the wound.

As determined, informed and feisty as she was, Sky had somehow remained an eternal optimist throughout these worst of times for humanity. For his father's grief to cause him to simply shut down was to insult their precious memories of her.

While Tony had looked up to his father his whole life, his sister had been his inspiration. If she had survived the raid, Sky would have been furious and devastated by their losses, but she would also have looked for any possible positives and whatever they might have learned, whatever they could do to better protect themselves. A natural pragmatist, she might even have looked for ways to make peace with the Dragons, find a way to trade and keep both communities safe.

His parents simply wouldn't discuss it with him and the frustration boiled in Tony's veins. They ignored every question or attempted discussion about her, as if she had never existed. Yet she had burned so brightly, so unforgettably in her twenty-one years. In his darkest moment, he wondered if Dan and Amanda Hightower might be secretly proud of their daughter's sacrifice.

It was Tony Hightower, the family's teenage son, who represented them at Sky's memorial ceremony.

His hands gripped the frame of the wooden board that listed all eleven victims of the Welsh Dragons' raid. It was a privilege to be chosen as the craftsman to inlay the board with his fine leatherwork edging, chosen even over his own father. He had been surprised, elated, when Highnam's Spokesperson had approached him to undertake the work.

The pride swelling in his chest deflated, however, when he looked at his parents, as they stood among the other villagers in the old orangery of Highnam Court.

Tony's father had done his best to train him, for all the infallibility he saw in him now. Whether it be exquisite leatherwork or trying to save your family from bandits, Dan had always told his son that preparedness was key.

They'd laughed together when he'd told a ten-year-old Tony to 'be the leather' as he explained how to judge the tanning process. Stretching the hide as it cured and dried could put you at one with the material, enabling manipulation into the perfect form.

And when talking of the threat of raiders, Dan had cautioned, 'People don't hurt each other just for the sake of it. Always put yourself in the other person's shoes. These people are starving and their families will die without food. That's why they're here – they don't hate us. And we don't hate them. Prepare well, and we can avoid people being hurt.'

Yet none of this could save Sky when the marauders came over the border from the valleys between Merthyr Tydfil and Aber-gavenny. All their defences had been in anticipating raiders – survivors – from the English towns: Cirencester, Gloucester, perhaps.

Looking down from the meeting hall's little stage into his parents' blank eyes, Tony still couldn't understand how they had closed down since the discovery of their daughter's body. His finger-nails dug into the wooden board. He wanted to bash them over the head with it, to wake them from their stupor, to provoke some kind of emotion from them. What was wrong with them? They just stood there, jointly clinging on to her Armulet.

Sky's talents had been with people; Tony's skill was in his hands. Apprenticed to his father almost from when he could walk, the youngest Hightower had yet to surpass his mentor's artisanal exper-tise... until now.

Dan had clearly spiralled into depression in the three weeks since the raid and their home had descended into sullen silence. Tony had felt the anger burning every time his father did speak, because it was never about Sky, or how they had lost her light. Nothing. Dan didn't even react to Tony's shouts and punching of the furniture. Both parents stoically carried on, as if nothing had happened.

His mother still tilled their vegetable patch, still cooked the meals, still cleaned the solar panels each day. His father stirred the tanning bark drum, scraped the cowhide with the fleshing knife, cut the leather into the template shapes for their various products. But they were just going through the motions. Neither helped Tony to understand his own grief, or his rage.

'Preparedness is key!' Tony had shouted at his father, three days after Sky's death. 'But only be prepared against attack from the east. What kind of half-brained defence plan is that?'

Dan's mouth had been hidden by his beard, his response barely a mumble.

Tony knew the logic: the small roads, thick forests and mountainous terrain that separated England from Wales had been considered good barriers – a poor attack route.

On the Welsh side, there were only small populations, even before the unravelling of society and the devastation of the Times of Malthus. And the opportunities to grow food back there, over Offa's Dyke, were at least as good as in Gloucestershire. Surely, they would not need to take the food of others?

It was the urban inhabitants that would be forced to steal, insisted Dan. Highnam had suffered attempts from the Cirencester Posse annually for the last five years, but they were usually beaten back with little harm. In the first ever attack by the Welsh Dragons, Sky – and ten others – were lost. His father deserved his fury.

Tony now thought of the work he had done, as he held the memorial plaque and the decorative leather edging he had made with such love.

The brother who had lost his sister had been driven. He had felt his hands move without direction or instruction to make the most beautiful object their village had seen, determined it would outlast everyone in Highnam. Sky would shine on forever.

He'd worked with the finest material they had available, the thin, soft skin from a fallow deer. It had not been lost on Tony that this one had been hunted in the very woods the Dragons would have passed through to reach Highnam and he'd wondered if they'd slain any deer en route, in the same grotesque way they had killed his sister.

Once the names had been gilt inlaid into the oak board, the addition of its leather decoration had been the final task.

He'd smiled through his tears, as he'd planned the artwork, measured the spaces, trimmed the coloured leather, punched its decorative patterning, delicately glued and invisibly pinned it in place. Every cut, every colour, every element looked lovelier than anything he'd previously created.

Although his father had continued to work in the beamhouse and tanyard, he'd steadfastly avoided the workshop where Tony was finishing the memorial board, finding other tasks to excuse his absence.

The silence of this lonely work had cut deep. Tony had missed his father's language of tongue clicks, used to communicate the standards of his craftsmanship. Every job Tony worked on before this had always come with a commentary of tuts and tsks and clicks. His work had never been perfect.

Often, even before Tony began to tap the embossing stamp or squeeze the awl or roll the cutting blade, Dan would give a sonorous tongue pop. There was no syntax or real vocabulary to this language, but father and son, master and apprentice, both understood each instruction for Tony to amend his action. The clicking had stopped the day Sky died.

As he wiped another tear from the bottom of the oak slab he was holding, Tony remembered her inimitable smile. Their parents had thought naming her Sky Hightower was amusing, a family in-joke that bound the four of them together.

Now, as he stood in the assembly room, he pictured her as she had been a decade earlier, in the branches of their apple tree, flaxen pigtails swaying, shouting to their mother, 'I'm Sky High! Up a wooden Tower!' His sister had descended into giggles at the top of the tree. Tony reckoned he'd been four or five when that earliest of memories was made.

Dedicating the memorial honours board was the opening part of this week's town meeting. With great reverence, and reining in his rage at his parents, Tony held up the leather-trimmed wooden board as another craftsman nailed it gently in place on the wall of the orangery. The names of the fallen were read aloud, and the gathering fell silent for two minutes.

The village Spokesperson moved on to the remaining business of the week's meeting. Still holding the board in place, Tony was stunned when his father was introduced as the first speaker. Confusion wrangled with his anger. He seethed as the slight, bearded man climbed up onto the dais.

The gathering hushed. Their head of security had not only failed them, he had also lost his own daughter. Voices caught in their throats as they craned their necks to hear what he might say.

But before Tony could berate his father publicly, Sky's irrepressible voice rang out in the cavernous room. Dan was holding up his daughter's Armulet as it played back a message. And Tony now heard the last words his sister had spoken before she was attacked. His knees wobbled, shocked at the sound of her voice. He held onto the only thing available to keep him from collapsing, the frame of the memorial board. As he gripped the leather he'd worked on so lovingly, Tony's stomach flipped somersaults.

'I want this on record. If Highnam used the audiopts, we'd have seen them coming ahead of time.' Sky sounded casual, mildly annoyed.

The room froze in silence, listening to a disembodied voice from beyond the grave, recognisable to every one of them, now rooted in place, statues of sadness and shame. Dan held the Armulet aloft, dangling by the leather strap he had made for his daughter.

'She asked you for this security system, and you said "No".' He almost shouted the last word, as if mimicking a rowdy mob. Employing oratorical flair Tony had never heard before, his father paused. The silence had the desired impact on the audience. Tony could feel it eating into their hearts.

'She came to this meeting six months ago and explained how this is the best possible security system, and you said 'No'. You said she was too young to know what Orwell had written. You even said she was too young to understand what it meant. You said we mustn't go back to the State having control over our every movement. For God's sake, people, there is no State! And because of your pig-headedness...' His purposeful voice cracked. 'I've lost her.' Dan fell to his knees. 'I'm so sorry, my beautiful girl. How could I let you down?'

After a minute on his hands and knees, he pulled himself up again. He pointed to the crowd. 'How dare you mourn these brave men and women, when she brought you the solution and you refused her?' His finger swung round towards Tony clinging on to the board.

He stood, raised up to his full height, and thundered at his neighbours, 'Now there is no Sky.' Dan caught his breath and continued, 'There is no Jackie. There is no Ravi. There is no Geeta. There is no Callum...'

Since its astonishing discovery, lying dormant on everyone's Armulet and in the network of cellphone towers, this all-pervasive surveillance system had since been successfully implemented in Hereford. Sky, who'd always been alert to any news on the grapevine that might be of use to her cherished community, brought this information to a town meeting in the autumn of 2037, expecting it would be the most obvious thing for Higham to adopt.

A venerable couple, teachers in the old days, had argued eloquently about personal privacy and the oppression of the State. The assembled throng on that day swayed in the current of their arguments but ultimately voted against Highnam implementing the audiopts.

Tony stepped across to interrupt his father, catching the hand Dan was using to point at the memorial board. He cried into the assembly hall: 'Why didn't we just accept the damn technology? My sister would still be alive today if we did!'

Tony now pointed at his dad. 'Be prepared – people will come. He told us all over and over. We tried but it wasn't enough – we must have a better system. Unless we want more of this.' He turned his hand towards the new sign. 'Do you want a whole wall of memorial boards?'

Meetings at Highnam were often easily influenced by high emotion. Voting intentions could swing back and forth several times before the Spokesperson called for a show of hands. The mood of the mob could shift, like the huge tides on the Severn and an idea could surge through the crowd like the mighty tidal bore wave that rushed up the river every six months. That wave now went to work on the crowd. From the back of the room, somebody began a chant. 'Use the audiopts! Turn it on! Use the audiopts! Turn it on!'

Within seconds the clamouring was cacophonous. The Spokesperson struggled to be heard. He waved both hands up and down and shouted to call a vote. 'Highnam to begin using the audiopt surveillance system as soon as possible?' Normally, resolutions were framed with more formality, but even the meeting's leader was caught up on the tidal bore wave of change.

Hands launched into the air, many people raising them in fists punching the air. They didn't even bother to count the votes. The audiopt surveillance system would protect Highnam for the future. Tony knew Sky would have celebrated this legacy.

Her parents now left the hall and walked hand-in-hand to Highnam Court's Victorian church and the graveyard where she lay, while their surviving child stared dumbfounded at their backs. They had not shared their grief with him at all, and yet, they had honoured his sister in the best possible way.

Find out more about this future England in the novels by Miles M Hudson:

The Times of Malthus, 2089 and *The Mind's Eye*

FAITH/FAITHFUL

A.B. KYAZZE

KATHMANDU AIRPORT ARRIVALS, WEEK 1, DAY 1

Monsoon season was supposed to be finished by now, according to the guidebooks, but they were wrong. Anna had just landed in Kathmandu, and she could feel it in every follicle. It was like electricity and humidity combined, hovering over her skin and all around. Overhead, the clouds were building up violent and opaque, blocking any view of the Himalayas.

'You've never left the country before.' Rupert poked fun at her when she was planning the trip. He was so smug, having spent a semester in India the year before. Even though she thought she loved him, his condescension was irritating. 'How are you going to cope? I bet you'll be all at sea.'

She was determined to prove him wrong. She could survive a little rain, for sure. But when it broke, it was like someone had dumped a bucket over her head, shoulders, and luggage. Nothing was untouched; no umbrella could be opened fast enough. Anna struggled to keep her eyes open wide, searching for any sign of her pen-pal Parvati, who had promised to meet her at Arrivals.

Taxis and banged-up mini-buses whirled into the lanes, decorated in bright colours and ornaments and bells that jangled with every bump. They honked in wild melodies as they pulled up and pulled away, undeterred by the downpour.

Anna had no working mobile phone, and no plan B. So it was a relief when she recognised Parvati from the photographs they had exchanged. She arrived at the airport in a motorcycle rickshaw that slowed but did not stop. Anna watched as she jumped out, side-stepping a large ditch in the process. She was small and thin, wearing a white salwar kameez that was soaked through in seconds. She carried an umbrella but then, just as suddenly as it came, the rain ceased. The percussion of the raindrops came to a halt, with the echoes leaving ripples in puddles all around.

Parvati looked up with a big smile, as her eyes caught Anna's from a distance. She raised her umbrella skyward and said, 'Welcome to Nepal!'

Anna had to laugh and waved as best she could with one hand, the other holding tight to her bags.

Parvati came closer, and gave a hug that surprised Anna. She spoke very fast with a learned British accent. 'We will take the group taxi, now that we are together and you have such things. I just took the motorcycle for its quickness. How was your flight? Was it fun?'

Anna struggled to think of how to describe it, knowing that Parvati had never been on a plane before. She came from a village near the border with India, where there was no running water, and her family lived in a house with mud floors. They would be sharing a small room for two weeks in Kirtipur, the university quarters, before visiting Parvati's family in the south for a wedding.

'My wedding,' Parvati said, not looking at Anna as they sat side by side in the back row of the still mini-bus, while the driver waited for more passengers before setting off.

'I can't believe you're getting married! Anna asked. 'When?'

'It's all arranged. We are happy to have your presence.'

'Arranged?' Anna asked carefully. 'Does that mean...'

'My family approves. His too.' Parvati's finger traced the stitching on the edge of her top.

'How long have you been planning this?'

'Since before we were born.' Parvati looked up with a slight smile. 'Do you have a boyfriend?'

'No,' Anna shook her head. It wasn't a lie, not now.

The minivan eventually filled with passengers, luggage and even a wide carton of square bird cages, providing clucking and feathers and the distinct smell of chicken poop. As the engine turned on, screeching singing came over the speakers.

'Bollywood,' Parvati leaned back in her seat and closed her eyes. 'My favourite.'

Anna couldn't go to sleep, not just yet. Her mind dashed between the last conversations with Rupert and what she was seeing out the window: the dirt road, busy with cars, taxis, motorcycles and animals. A pothole the size of a cow loomed ahead, and she wondered how deep it was. Then a real cow pushed in from the side of the road, and she saw that the pothole was actually wider, in comparison. The cow was brown and skinny, with small horns and bones protruding from the hips and shoulders.

Cows were sacred here, she knew, due to their place in the Hindu religion. Cars swerved around the beast, and honked at each other to make room. The animal itself seemed mildly confused, but not alarmed, as it put its head down to sniff something in the mud.

The minivan lurched to the right to make room for the cow, and then back again. The patterns of giving way and taking charge here didn't make sense in Anna's mind, but maybe that's also because she was used to driving on the other side of the road.

'Traffic is chaos here,' Parvati said. 'You'll get used to it.'

WASHINGTON D.C., THREE DAYS EARLIER

'It just seems really... ' Anna searched for the right words, but gave up... 'Messy,' was the best she could come up with. She blew over the top of her coffee, which was freshly brewed and too hot to sip.

'Don't be so repressed, Anna.' Rupert put an extra sachet of sugar into his latté. He often complained that his blood sugar was dropping, needed a pick-me-up. 'It's just a different way of looking at love, that's all. You need to open your mind.'

When Anna opened her mind, she didn't like what she saw. Rupert dancing away from her at a club. Anna going home by herself, sleeping alone. Rupert coming over the next morning in rumpled clothing, smelling of sweat and cigarettes. And him repeating a phrase she never liked to hear: 'You just don't understand how hard it is for someone like me to be faithful to one person.'

She tried to understand. But really, it didn't feel hard. It felt messed up. He was here sometimes, but then he was gone, back with his ex. A butterfly, someone once called him, and not in a good way. Flitting back and forth between sources of nectar. She gave an involuntary shudder.

'Just because it's not the way you think about things, doesn't mean that it can't work.' He reached out and put his hand over hers. The cafeteria table felt sticky under her palm, and she wanted to slip out from underneath.

'I don't know. Sounds... chaotic.'

'Chaos can be beautiful. It can be creative and open. Love can be like that.'

'I don't think so. I need a bit more of a sense of... order.'

'You're always trying to control things.' He withdrew his hand and crossed his arms in front of his chest. 'You can't ask me to change who I am. Can't you just see that?'

She shook her head and pushed back the chair. She left him there, with the coffee that would have burned her tongue.

Nepal, week 3, day 1

Another bus, another destination: Down to the Terai, to Parvati's family home for the wedding. Anna was reluctant to leave the capital, with the markets and temples and bookstores and orchestrated craziness of traffic, but she knew she needed to go and support her friend.

In the two weeks they had been sharing a room, Parvati tried to convince Anna that this was a love marriage, as they called it. They had known each other since they were babies, born in the same village to mothers who were distant cousins. Despite the sense of predestination, Parvati assured Anna that it was love.

'But what you'll see in the village will seem quite different.' On the bus she cupped her hand to speak into Anna's ear, to avoid being overheard. 'I will have to act as though it's not free will. As if I don't want to get married, and I am being pushed to leave my family home. It's all an act, with tears and everything. But that doesn't mean it's forced. I promise you.' Parvati sat back and gave an assured nod. 'I am a modern woman, and he knows I will finish my university studies before we have a family. He is a good man, working in Delhi. If I want to go and be with him after graduation, this is the only way.'

Parvati pointed out the landmarks in the distance, ones that Anna could barely distinguish due to the dust from the roads and cars. The landscape was flattening out, as they came closer to the border with India. The chaos and colours of the capital were far behind.

'I am named after the goddess of fertility, love and devotion,' Parvati continued softly. 'He can't change it, he has to be faithful. Once we are committed, that's it.'

Even though doubts tried to creep in the margins of her mind, Anna was a little jealous of how sure Parvati seemed. Maybe it was blind faith, but sure, all the same.

WEEK 4, DAY 3

Another bus ride, this time up into the mountains. After these weeks in Nepal, she had grown accustomed to the jolting motion of the buses, the Bollywood music and the constant horns honking in passing. There were some scary near-misses, and the stories of past disasters whirled around her head. The carcasses of vehicles that had never made it home, crumpled and rusted at the side of the road, did little for her confidence in the driving.

But she tried to take control and dampen down those thoughts. She kept the memories of the elaborate Hindu wedding front-of-mind, as she made her way to the foothills of the Himalayas.

Anna had enjoyed the whole week immensely. During the preparations she was welcomed into the family and into the kitchen, with the smell of cumin and cloves. All the aunties and married cousins were there gossiping, knowing she wouldn't understand, but she didn't mind. Parvati's brothers were busy bringing in the goats from the fields, and Parvati's younger sisters were on their hands and knees, repainting the floors with mud and cow dung before the big day.

Anna was a faithful friend and stood by Parvati. Anna wore a borrowed sari, bright in yellow and orange. It was tight around the waist with an extensive number of folds that Parvati's oldest Aunt insisted on redoing just before the ceremony.

Parvati had told the truth. At first, she'd played the part of an anguished daughter, clinging to her parents and sisters the night before the ceremony. But at the actual wedding, with the whirlwind of red and gold, the drumming, the cheering, the crowds and the feasting, it was all different. Parvati was celebrated, elevated, and smiling widely. In the last stage, as the bride and groom circled each other at the centre of the crowd, and then fed each other rice with their hands, Anna was convinced that they were united with happiness. With what felt like the whole village, Parvati was joyous. Sure of herself, confident and beloved.

Anna had stood by, cheering and clapping with the family, and she was storing up memories to tell someone later. But for who? Rupert was the one she used to tell everything, to make him laugh or to hear his views. She used to care about his opinions, but there was no longer that obligation to tell him, or for him to listen when she came back home. However, the absence of somebody was still a feeling, palpable at moments. She tried to push him out of her mind, and just be there for Parvati.

And now Anna was travelling for another celebration – the Buddhist full moon ceremony. As planned, she was heading alone to the foothills for a weekend of silent meditation. She had booked accommodation at a Buddhist nunnery in the foothills near Pokhara, hoping it would be just the thing to settle her mind and help her focus.

She found the retreat centre by nightfall. The doorway was marked with candles burnt down to thick stubs on either side of the stairs. In contrast to the previous weeks, this was a place of silent retreat. The Buddhist nun who opened the door pointed to a calligraphed list of rules in multiple languages: No talking, no laughter, no smoking, no alcohol, no meat. Otherwise, you would be asked to leave.

Anna nodded and was led down dark-wooded hallways to her room. With just a simple bed and a maroon robe, along with slippers to move silently along the polished floors, it had everything she needed.

In the morning, at first Anna couldn't remember where she was. Then her eyes settled on the light coming in through her window, with the smell of porridge faintly seeping in, and she smiled. This was supposed to be her 'me' time, to settle her mind and move towards having a calm heart. To make sense of the excitement she had seen over the recent weeks, and discover who she was, away from the noise and busyness of normal life. She knew that wouldn't all happen in a couple of days. But maybe it would give her the beginnings of something she could hold onto.

She changed into her robe and emerged from her room, following others just ahead. They came to a dining room where about sixty women sat cross-legged on the floor at low round tables, eating a milky rice porridge. There was no cutlery, but Anna was now used to the practice of drinking from a bowl and eating rice with her hands. She tried not to make eye contact with people, so as to avoid any risk of conversation.

A large white woman came out of a swinging door. She had mid-length grey hair cut flat over her brows, accentuating her square jaw and the circles below her eyes. She wore an apron over her robes, and wiped her hands on it as she surveyed the room before going back into the kitchen.

The day passed very slowly. With no verbal instructions, and no companionship, Anna followed the signals and the gestures of others. Her mind was stubborn, though, not wanting to relinquish old habits of darting about.

They sat for hours in the lotus position, focusing on a candle. The colours in the flame reminded her of Parvati's sari the morning after the wedding, a delicious golden yellow. Anna wondered what her friend was doing now, and if she was happy in her newly-married state.

Then there was a silent slow walking meditation in a large circle with many others. Anna tried to concentrate on every breath and the feeling of her feet on the hard ground. It wasn't enough to hold her imagination, and her thoughts flew to Washington, to Rupert, and to their last conversation. She tried not to think about what he was doing now, or who he was with.

Through her peripheral vision, she saw nuns doing chores such as gardening or washing the windows. Others were locked inside their thoughts, concentrating and facing inward. Anna thought she would probably be an active kind of nun, if she could ever make it that far in the quest for a still mind.

She tried to treat herself with kindness, not sharp criticism. She watched her thoughts dart about between memories of Kathmandu, thinking about Parvati's love match, and also regrets about Rupert slipped in. But not too many. She was already feeling as though there were more than miles between her and him, some shift in perspective.

He was too harsh on her, and worse: his chaotic love was not the kind she needed. She would never go back to that, to him. But where she thought she would feel angry or triumphant, she just felt... empty. As if part of her, her emotions related to him, had been exhaled into the air.

Dinner was another no-talking affair, but it was easier, after spending a day alongside these women. The clear vegetable soup with solid dumplings wasn't filling, but Anna found she didn't have huge cravings for food after such a quiet day.

A clang and smash came from the behind the kitchen door, and before anyone moved, they heard a strong northern British accent swear '*Bloody* hell!'

Giggles came up from some of the nuns, the younger ones who couldn't help it. Those closest to the swinging door dashed in to see what had happened, and Anna went too.

The large white woman, the cook, was on her hands and knees next to a toppled cauldron, with the contents emptied all over the floor. She was surrounded by nuns swirling around with mops and towels, as they tried to contain a greasy broth and push it towards a drain.

'Sorry everyone,' the woman was saying, even as silence was supposed to be the order of the day. 'It's just so frustrating!' She reached up to the stove to try to pull herself to her feet, but touched the burner; although it was off, it was still hot, and she shouted again, 'Dammit!'

The senior nun placed a stern hand on the woman's arm.

'I'm just not made for this,' the cook said, and pushed out a side door into the garden.

Anna followed, wondering if she could help.

The sun was just falling past the mountains to the northwest. The jagged icy peaks traced a line like molten silver. Anna drew a sharp breath and rubbed her arms over her bare shoulders.

A few clicks, and the British woman lit up a cigarette. When Anna stared in astonishment, she said, 'Don't look at me like that.'

She flicked her hand through her hair like she was freeing herself from something. 'The nuns are asking too much, all this silence and conformity. They should know that we can only be who we really are. People don't change much, even if they want to.'

Low clunky bells chimed from behind the building, and the woman spoke again. 'Cows?' she said. 'Up here?'

A train of the animals, all wearing bells on their collars, moved slowly into view at the back of the garden. About two dozen of them stomped a path along the edge of the foothills. They were faithfully followed by a teenage boy, swinging a stick and singing loudly.

'I could just murder a burger right now, couldn't you?' the woman said.

Anna started to laugh. She tried to keep it quiet at first, but the way she had been holding everything inside all day made it impossible. It exploded outwards forcefully, spreading past her body into the mountain air. It mixed with the sounds of the cook's laughter and the cows and the boy's singing and the memories of a tumultuous month.

The door to the kitchen opened, and the senior nun looked out at them, determining the source of the voices and laughter.

With little warning, an aberrant late monsoon rain began to fall. Tentatively at first, and then more insistent. Anna held her hands over her head and tried to stifle her emotions, but the tears from the laughter and the rain mixed as they ran down her cheeks.

The cook shook her head at first, whether in disbelief or displeasure, Anna couldn't tell. But her expression was one of good humour. She stretched out her arms as she defiantly held out her cigarette with a glowing orange tip. Shaking her head stronger now, she twirled around in circles. Her grey hair and maroon robes flowed out in cone shapes, rising with her motion. She had nothing to lose now that the rules had been broken.

BEFORE YOU GO

The book you are holding in your hand is the result of our dreams to be authors. We hope you enjoyed our stories as much as we enjoyed writing them. They exist through dedication, passion and love.

Reviews help persuade readers to give this book a shot. You are helping the community discover and support new writing. It will take *less than a minute* and can be *just a line* to say what you liked or didn't. Please leave us a review wherever you bought this book from. A big thank you on behalf of all our authors in the *Breakthrough Books* collective.

About the Authors

Eli Allison wants to tell you that she's always wanted to be a writer, but that's a lie. She wanted to be a hat maker, a florist; there was a summer she flirted with the idea of being a sandwich merchant, a rally driver and a gymnast — every single Olympic season. She's still hopeful that last one will pan out, so if she's called up, this middle-aged woman will dump the writer's life for roly–polies in sparkly spanks. For Britain! When she's not dreaming of gold, she writes weird sci-fi. And eats cheese.
eli-allison.com
Instagram: eli_allison3

Mark Bowsher is a proudly dyspraxic writer and filmmaker from Kent. His short story 'The Hunger Wall' was published in the Fish Publishing Anthology 2023. His debut novel, YA fantasy 'The Boy Who Stole Time', was published in 2018 by Unbound. He made three award-winning short films and 14 documentaries for Dan Snow's History Hit. He lives in Bristol and enjoys board games, travelling the world, swimming and long walks where he can conjure up exciting new adventures. www.rabbitislandpro.co.uk
Twitter: @markbowsherfilm

Stephanie Bretherton is an author and copywriter with a passion for the power of words, nature and science. A lifelong nomad and storyteller (in one medium or another) she now lives on a cliff in far

west Cornwall. Her well-received, Kindle-bestselling novel *Bone Lines* will soon be followed by book two in *The Children of Sarah* series.
www.stephaniebretherton.com

Jamie Chipperfield is a full-time carer currently living in Cornwall. This anthology is his second time in print.
Twitter: @jchipperfield3

Sue Clark feels she's found her true calling as a writer of contemporary comic fiction, after a varied career as a BBC comedy scriptwriter, journalist, copywriter, editor and PR. Her debut novel, *Note to Boy*, was published in 2020. Her second, *A Novel Solution*, will be released in March 2024. A third is, as they say, currently on the stocks; author-speak for giving her sleepless nights.
www.sueclarkauthor.com
X, formerly Twitter: @sueclarkauthor

Jason Cobley was born in Devon of Welsh parents. He is now an over-caffeinated teacher with high blood pressure and a few books to his name. This includes *A Hundred Years to Arras*, a pastoral war novel set in France in 1917. He now lives and ruminates in Warwickshire.
jmcobley.wordpress.com

Stevyn Colgan is an artist, musician, speaker, lecturer and author of ten books. He was, for a decade, one of the primary writers of the BBC TV show 'QI' and was on the writing team that won the Rose D'Or for Radio 4's 'The Museum of Curiosity'.

Samuel Dodson is an award-winning writer and editor based in London, UK. He is the founder of creative collective, Nothing in the Rulebook. His first book, *Philosophers' Dogs*, was published by Unbound in 2021.
www.samuel-dodson.com

Twitter: @instantidealism

Miles Hudson loves words and ideas. He's also a physics teacher, surfer, author, hockey player, inventor, backpacker and idler. Miles has published The Audiopts Series which includes the novels *The Times of Malthus, 2089* and *The Mind's Eye* and The Penfold Detective Mysteries which includes *The Cricketer's Corpse, The Kidney Killer* and *Burns Night Burns*. Born in Minneapolis, Miles has lived in Durham in northern England for 35 years. https://mileshudson.com and @MilesMHudson on Facebook and @mileshudsonauthor on TikTok

A.B. Kyazze is an author and photographer who worked around the world before settling in London. She has published many short stories and two novels, *Into the Mouth of the Lion* (2021) and *Ahead of the Shadows* (2022). A third novel is due out in 2024. She also runs creative workshops exploring the senses, and is a Trustee for a fantasy writing charity. www.abkyazze.com

Pete Langman was diagnosed with Parkinson's in 2008, at the tender age of 40, since when he has taught at several universities, written *Killing Beauties, The Country House Cricketer* and *Slender Threads: a young person's guide to Parkinson's Disease,* and provided copy for all manner of other publications. His next foray into publishing will be *Spycraft,* a work of history co-authored with his partner, Professor Nadine Akkerman, released into the wild in June 2024. www.petelangman.com and @elegantfowl

Virginia Moffatt has written two novels *Echo Hall* (Unbound) and *The Wave* ((Harper One More Chapter) and a flash fiction collection *Rapture and What Comes After* (Gumbo Press). She is currently working on a couple of new novels and a novella. She lives in Dorset with her husband Chris.

Maybe it's because he's from Ireland that **Eamon Somers** loves writing stories with unreliable narrators. He says they often reveal more of life's truths than their more respectable cousin narrators. His debut novel Dolly Considine's Hotel clearly shows that in the area of lies and gross exaggeration Eamon has form.
eamonsomers.com

Nicole Swengley is a London-based, freelance journalist who has written for the Financial Times, the Telegraph, The Times and Wall Street Journal amongst many other publications. Her short stories have featured in women's magazines and a crime anthology (Pavilion). She is currently working on her debut novel, a contemporary thriller with a strong art history thread.

Damon L. Wakes has been writing one story a day every July since 2012, making for a total of 372 at the time of writing and possibly quite a lot more by the unknowable future time in which you are reading this. He is also the author of *Ten Little Astronauts* - a sci-fi reimagining of Agatha Christie's *And Then There Were None* - and *Face of Glass*, a prehistoric fantasy novel. His other work tends towards the experimental, ranging from virtual reality games to procedurally generated religious texts, and occasionally involves wiring fresh bananas into other people's computers.
damonwakes.wordpress.com

P J Whiteley is an author of fiction and non-fiction. *Close of Play*, his first novel, received a review by the Church Times which stated that it was 'well written, but above all, well observed', while the follow-up *Marching on Together* received a cover quote from Louis de Bernières. *A Love of Two Halves* was described by SJ Bradley, editor of the literary journal *Strix*, as 'an uplifting northern novel'.
www.pjwhiteley.com

Also by Breakthrough Books

Taking Liberties, a highly regarded anthology of short stories on the theme of freedom.

Praise for *Taking Liberties*

"A cornucopia of delights. From the very first story I was struck by the skill and literary nature of the writing. Many have plots that would translate brilliantly into television dramas or films, with so much packed into them. An intelligent, carefully crafted and rewarding collection with something for every reader." — Linda Hill, Linda's Book Bag

"Although very different, the stories are all extremely well written and elicit a plethora of emotions in the reader. All of human life is here, and you will be delighted by the variety of approaches the writers have taken." — Julie Morris, A Little Book Problem

"A brilliant collection of short stories and slices of life that will stay with you, and leave you wanting more!" — Ste Sharp, author

In Truth, Madness, a novel by TV reporter, Imran Khan, about a war correspondent on a journey of awakening that drives him to the edge of sanity.

Praise for *In Truth, Madness*

"A Neil Gaiman style spectacular set across the ancient and present day Middle East."— Laury Silvers, author of *The Sufi Mysteries Quartet*

"A beautifully written, magical tale of mental health and international news." — Dareen Abughaida, principal anchor for Al Jazeera English

"Unusual. Intriguing... I couldn't put it down." — Barbara Mainville, book critic.

"Funny, clever, relatable and deeply moving." — Horia El Hadad, documentary maker

ACKNOWLEDGMENTS

The very nature of a 'collective' means there are so many people to thank, but particularly all the authors included here, who have not only contributed their talent and creativity in producing each story, but many other valuable skills in producing this book. Their support and encouragement of each other, plus critical feedback at various stages, can't be measured.

Heartfelt thanks are also due to Zena Barrie for her time and objective editorial overview, the multi-talented Eli Allison for our cover design, and the collective's inexhaustible Renaissance woman, Ivy Ngeow, for typesetting (and unfailing common sense.)

Thanks also to Stephanie Bretherton and Philip Whiteley who wrestle with the 'business end' of the publishing company, attempting to shape order from the chaos without sacrificing its gifts of literary emergence. And to Jamie Chipperfield, for so many things, but mostly just for being Jamie.